THE MUD-HUT DWELLERS

THE
MUD-HUT
DWELLERS

By Mihail Sadoveanu

TWAYNE PUBLISHERS, INC.

NEW YORK

THE MUD-HUT DWELLERS

Nita Lepadatu arrived at Iliseni, on the estate of the boyar George Avrameanu, alone and carrying nothing but his hooded cloak and a polished cudgel. It was autumn. He appeared from somewhere beyond the hill, climbed towards the barns, and there stopped to survey the pond at his feet and the manor house itself.

All around, and as far as he could see, there were only open fields—behind him into the far distance whence he had come, and to the east as far as the river Prut. He had walked many miles without passing a single human habitation. In those days the Jijia and Prut regions were nothing but deserts.

Nita slipped between the barns. In one of the sheds voices could be heard and the rhythmic sound of winnowers at work. A lean horse, tethered in a dark corner, stood motionless, its head down as it dozed in the autumn sunshine. A white dog with a shaggy coat leaped out and began barking furiously at the stranger's legs.

Lepadatu held him off with his cudgel and advanced slowly towards the shed from which he could hear the dull thumping of the winnowers.

7

"What's up there?" asked a thin voice like the bleat of a lamb.

A little old man, bareheaded, with untidy hair, came out of the shed. "What is it? . . . Down, Coltun!" he shouted at the dog, bending towards it. "Get out! Off with you! Go to your place, you brute!" He picked up a bit of wood and threw it at the dog, chasing it away. Then he turned towards Nita Lepadatu and looked at him searchingly.

"Hm . . . well, well!" he said, somewhat surprised. "Lad, you're not from these parts. I've never seen you before. . . . What do you want?"

"You're right," answered the wayfarer. "I come from a long way off, from down there. . . ."

"Did anybody send you here?"

"Nobody. Only, if you don't mind, may I ask who is the owner of this estate? You think I'll manage to get work here?"

"It's all right, lad," bleated the old man in his thin voice. "If you come here you'll have plenty to do. The estate is big. As for the master, he has a good heart."

"But what's his name?"

"Mr. George . . . that's his name, Mr. George Avrameanu. You go up to the house and talk to him."

"Good," murmured Nita Lepadatu.

The old man examined him with his sparkling little eyes.

The stranger was weary, his face dark with the dust of the roads. He looked sadly into space with his green eyes, deep-sunken below his brow and bushy eyebrows. He had not shaved for many days, but his curly, drooping moustache did not cover his mouth. His lips were dry and scorched; from time to time he half-opened them, passing his tongue over their surface to moisten them.

"I'm thirsty," he said with an effort. "Be so good to give me a mug of water."

"Of course!" answered the old man. "I should be sinning if I didn't give you some. Come to the hut."

His face became friendly.

"They call me Nastase Tentea," he said with a laugh as they went together towards the hut. "I have lived in these parts for a long time. Three masters — grandfather, father, and son — found me here and left me here. . . . Oh, I've given drinks to plenty of weary lads like you. I've given them drinks so that I shan't thirst when I get to the next world."

He walked with short steps, his pigskin sandals crunching on the dusty ground. The wind blew out the thick cotton shirt which was too big for his small frail body. The great, high barns and the shed where men were winnowing and sieving the heaps of corn were left behind.

Uncle Nastase Tentea led Lepadatu to his hut half-buried in the ground, going in first down a step or two.

The wayfarer followed him into a tiny clay-plastered room, in the corner of which was a hearth whose chimney passed through the earthen roof.

Along the sides of the room were wooden benches covered with rough woollen matting and, at the end, a round opening in which a bit of glass had been cleverly inserted

9

to make a window so small that there was barely room to peer through it. Light entered mainly through the doorway.

Near the hearth, on a low three-legged stool, sat a girl of about twenty, trying to light a fire of maize husks.

When the old man and Nita came in she looked around, showing surprise at the sight of the stranger; mechanically she smoothed her print skirt and cotton blouse, and then smiled.

"Good-day," said Nita Lepadatu, his eyes resting on her.

"Good-day . . ."

Uncle Nastase looked for the bucket behind the door. He kicked it with his sandal and murmured in his shrill voice. "Hm . . . well, well! a great big girl—and an empty bucket! Take the bucket, Marghiolita, and fill it so that a weary wayfarer can have a drink."

"I'm going, father," replied the girl hurriedly and rather shamefacedly. She took the bucket and went out with downcast eyes.

"Hm . . . well, well!" said uncle Nastase, good-humoredly this time. "She's my only child; as for my wife, I don't know what has become of her. She went off one fine day, twelve or thirteen years ago, and I've never heard of her since. She's a good worker, my little girl, but she gets bored staying here alone all day. . . . We haven't any church to go to on Sundays. Not like what I've seen down there on the Siret, or on the Moldova, where there isn't a village without a priest or church. . . . You might say that there's another sort of people down there. Here, with us, there is even no dancing. When I was a youngster I lived

in other places, here and there, and I know that respectable folk used to invite others in for dancing. But here we
have no respectable folk at all. Here we live as we can . . .
by God's grace. So, you understand, she's like everybody
is . . . she'd like to enjoy herself too while she's still young.
But how can she enjoy herself here, in this hut of mine?"

"I see," said Lepadatu, sitting down on the bench with
a sigh.

"Hm . . . well, well!" went on the old man. "Here you
become a savage. Even my daughter has grown up like a
savage. . . . It's true that now and then she goes to the
manor house and that the ladies there have taught her a
bit how to carry herself and talk. And she's been once or
twice to the town, to Saveni, but that's all. How can you
expect her to know about anything?"

"Folk live as they can," remarked Nita Lepadatu quietly.

"Hm . . . well, well! That's true. . . . Look at me now. I
feel a sort of joy at anybody coming here . . . at having
someone to exchange a word or a thought with. Do you
come from far? from the south?"

"Yes, from the south . . . but not from very far."

"Perhaps you come from the town of Iasi? . . ."

"Oh, no! Iasi is far off. I've never been there. I'm only
a poor fellow, an orphan, I've no family."

"Hm . . . well, well!" sighed uncle Nastase, getting up.
"Here's the girl coming back with the water."

Here she was, indeed, hurrying, rather breathless, her
bare feet making a plashing sound. Her big eyes were
shining in her dark face. She went down the two steps,
into the hut, then to the hearth to fetch a little earthen-

11

ware cup which she filled with water and handed to the wayfarer.

Nita Lepadatu drank it off at one gulp and asked for another. He drank this too, then wiped his lips and moustache with his shirt-sleeve. He gave the earthen jug to the girl and, feeling invigorated, said, by way of thanks:

"How good the water is here! May God give you good health—and all your heart's desire . . ."

"Hm . . . well, well!" remarked the old man. "Nothing in this world is better than water."

The girl smiled softly. She put the bucket back behind the door and returned to sit down by the hearth on her three-legged stool. Nita Lepadatu noticed that her cheeks seemed redder and her hair softer and smoother. She had no doubt looked at herself in the stream and freshened her face and hair with a drop of clear water.

"What am I going to do now?" asked the wayfarer with a sigh.

"Hm . . . well, well! What are you going to do? First of all you're going to have a bite with us . . . aren't we human? After that we'll go down as far as the manor. I think you'll stay with us, for Mr. George always needs hands."

"He needs men for the cattle," put in Marghiolita, who was sitting near the hearth.

"How do you know that?" inquired the old man, his voice even higher, shaking his head and laughing.

"I heard them say down there when I was at the house."

"Hm . . . well, well! She's right. They will need a man for the cattle," the old man concluded with conviction.

Nita Lepadatu was worn out after his long journey and

the droughty wind, but the fresh water, the rest in the hut, and the meal prepared by the old man's daughter made him feel better.

He too began to talk of one thing and another, of another boyar he had known and of his estate, and of the place he himself came from; then he let uncle Nastase tell his stories, so as to be able to look at the girl. He already had the feeling that he was among friends in this hut.

SHORTLY before sundown they went out and made their way towards the manor house. From the threshold the girl watched them as they left. She thought that the wayfarer, if there were no way of his being taken on, would go off on his wanderings without coming back to the hut to see her. She felt a sort of tightening of the heart. By his eyes and voice he seemed a gentle, peaceful man. She would have liked him to come back and sit down again on the bench, looking at her lingeringly and asking her for another drink of cold water.

In the west the sun was sinking behind the mass of hills, in a light flurry of clouds. The dry wind was still blowing across the plain. As far as the eye could see there were ploughed stubble fields and maize fields. The water of a quiet pool glimmered in a hollow of the landscape. A hillock rose with a tangle of dark brambles. There was no sign of woods, orchards, or villages. Above this stretch of country the sky was a whitish vault of solitude.

The two men advanced slowly along a narrow, dusty path. Their steps sent up a cloud of dust which the wind seized at once and drove to rest on the stubble and the high tufts of weeds growing on the boundaries between the maize fields.

A flight of rooks and starlings, lazily carried by the wind, rose from behind the barn, then disappeared into a valley.

"Hm . . . well, well! We're just getting to the manor," said the old man after a while. "Today is Saturday, and the boyar must be at home. On Saturday he comes in earlier from the fields."

"Is the estate big?" inquired Lepadatu.

"What?" Uncle Nastase gave the lad a look of amazement. "As far as your eyes can see and even farther. This estate is awfully big! It's the biggest estate in all the world! If it was any bigger how could the boyar get it worked, and how could he look after it? Once I asked him, "Mr. George, what do you do with so much land and so much money?"

"And what did he answer?"

"What did he answer? Hm . . . well, well! He didn't answer at all. He burst out laughing."

The lad shook his head and smiled. The old peasant smiled too, shaking his long hair, then, pointing with his dry and blackened fingers, announced:

"There, that's the boyar's home down there, and the outhouses."

There it was, near the pond, a white house, low, built of round logs, amid a huddle of thatched sheds and stables.

"'He has a splendid house, the boyar has," said uncle Nastase. "The boyars are used to having plenty of rooms.

15

. . . Another time I asked him: 'Mr. George, why do you need four such big rooms? What do you do with them?' "

"What did he say?"

"Hm . . . well, well! What could he say? He said nothing. He just laughed."

On a slope slightly steeper than the others, not far from the boyar's house, there was a long line of huts. Some were constructed in the way these huts usually are, half-buried and covered with beaten earth. The others were hollowed out of the very side of the ravine, and blocked with planks or wattle fences covered with a thin coat of clay which was flaking off already. Cloudlets of smoke issued from all these half-buried huts.

Here and there the glass pane of a skylight, not much bigger than a hand, reflected the slanting rays of the sun. There were no enclosures anywhere.

Cattle and pigs herded pell-mell at the doors. Hens scratched the dung, and rubbish heaped up on the roofs of the huts like dirty, ragged fur-caps.

"It's here the mud-hut dwellers live," said the old man. "These are the people we work the estate with."

"From what I see, the boyar has plenty of hands, that he has. . . ."

"Hm . . . well, well! plenty, of course. What did you think? Where you come from did the boyars not have so many? You see, our boyar owns the biggest estate. So he got people brought from everywhere. From time to time some leave, others take their place. . . . When the work is in full swing he brings them from places where villages are not so rare, and there are more people . . . but we al-

16

ways do all the heavy work with the people of the huts."

"Hm, it was like that with us," muttered Lepadatu. "I too was born in a mud-hut like these, and I grew up in one."

"Hm . . . well, well! In a hut like these . . . but in other parts people live in real houses. How I wonder what the winters are like out there. I once asked the boyar: 'Mr. George, in our huts we don't worry about the winter. But how is it you aren't cold in your big house?'"

"And what did he say?"

"What do you think he said? He just laughed. He said he had fires lit. How should I know?"

"That's how it is, uncle Nastase. People like us live half underground, half outside. You know very well we sometimes have terrible winters. We stay in the fields with the animals. It's because we're used to everything. As for the boyar, what would you expect? He's the boyar and he's got different habits."

"He's got another sort of a skin," added uncle Nastase.

This remark set them both laughing. They went down still farther and passed in front of the huts. Several men, clothed in miserable rags, were coming and going, watering cattle, leading horses by the bit, taking turns at a drinking well that worked by a balancing plank.

"Has the boyar come back?" the old man called to them.

"Yes, he's back," replied somebody's hoarse voice.

"That's good," murmured uncle Nastase as if to himself.

The manor house itself was not fenced around. People swarmed among the outhouses. Stablemen were leading horses to their stables. Behind the house a herd of cattle passed, raising thick clouds of dust skywards. The voices of the cattle men resounded ceaselessly, calling, shouting, threatening. From time to time a more furious volley of curses could be heard, and the sound of clubs beating down on the beasts' backs.

Invisible cattle bells tinkled sadly in the dust-cloudy air.

"See what our boyar's got in the way of cattle!" observed the old man, not without a touch of pride.

They went around the low log house and stopped at the back door. They waited a good while. Behind panes of the veranda the shadow of a woman showed from time to time.

"She's the one who keeps house for the boyar," whispered uncle Nastase.

The shadow passed once more. This time, however, it stopped and opened the door. A thin little woman appeared, pale, with coal-black eyes and a very sharp nose. She wore dark clothes, and a dark kerchief was carefully arranged to cover her hair.

"What is it, uncle Nastase?" she asked in a shrill voice.

"We should like to speak to the boyar."

"All right. But why do you never send your daughter to me now? We have a lot of work to do here, and she could help us."

"Who, Marghiolita?" said the old man, softly. "She's had some work to do at home. But I will send her along to you. Why not?"

"And what have you got to say to the boyar, if you please?" asked the little woman, her voice even shriller and speaking very fast.

18

"It's this lad here who would like a word with him."

The housekeeper gave Nita Lepadatu a sharp look and shut the door with a bang.

"Hm . . . well, well!" smiled uncle Nastase. "There, that's our nun. She behaves as sharply as she talks."

"What nun?" asked the lad in surprise.

"Why, this one. She came from a convent and now she keeps house for the boyar. How quick she is! That's how she always speaks. She wants us to feel that it's she who runs the house. Otherwise she hasn't a bad heart. She sometimes gossips with Marghiolita and tells her about herself. There's nothing to be done about it. Well, anyway, it wasn't a great deal of happiness that drove her to live in this desert."

The housekeeper passed again, even faster than before, like a flash of black across the panes of the veranda. Then they heard the sound of a man's step, and the boyar opened the door.

The two men uncovered their heads. Mr. George Avrameanu, young and strong-built, with a kind, jolly, and sunburnt face, stood before them, his hands in his trouser pockets, and looked at them. He smiled.

"Well, uncle Nastase," he said in a husky, rather drawling voice. "What's new?"

"What do you expect to be new, Mr. George? Up to now, everything's all right."

"Really?" replied the boyar gaily, jingling his keys in his trouser pocket. "What wind brings you here? Why did you leave the barns unattended?"

"But I haven't left them unattended, Mr. George. There

are still trustworthy folks down there. And then I count on my daughter . . ."

"What? How can you count on your daughter? But, who is this man? What do you want, both of you?"

"This?" said uncle Nastase, turning his head and looking at Nita as if he were seeing him for the first time. "A lad who came to our place today . . ."

"What's his name?"

Uncle Nastase did not answer but again turned to the young man and nodded to him. The stranger, turning his crumpled hat in his hands, answered:

"Nita Lepadatu."

The old man nodded and seemed to think that it was the first time he ever heard the lad's name and found it rather queer.

"Nita Lepadatu?" repeated the boyar. "Where do you come from?"

"From Negoiesti."

"Iasi district? And what do you want?"

"He would like to be taken on for the cattle, Mr. George," put in uncle Nastase.

"So he'd like to be taken on for the cattle, would he? Good. Have you any references?"

"No, I haven't any," said Nita. "Out there nobody asks for them."

"Is that how it is? In that case I won't ask you for any either . . . on condition you behave decently. But why did you leave the boyar from Negoiesti?"

"Mr. George, Sir, don't think I'm a bad man," Nita replied in a low voice. "It's true I'm poor, there's no doubt about it . . . I've no parents, no family, I haven't got a roof over my head . . . I've got nothing except these arms—but they can work—and I'm honest. I stayed ten years with the boyar at Negoiesti and I got a boy's wage. . . . I did think that now I could be paid like a man, and I asked for a raise in my wages. He didn't want to give it, and I left. I'm sorry. I had worked for ten years like a slave. But what could I do? I thought I should somehow find a bit of bread in this wide world. I set off last night and I walked and walked till I got here. If you will have me, Sir, I will be a faithful servant."

Mr. George listened to him in silence, turning his keys round and round in his trouser pocket. The virgin land that he was now clearing was always worked by rabble of this sort. It was with them that he increased his herds, that he got the corn in before sending it to Galati. In an isolated and desert region like this what he needed was hands. Whence they came, to whom they belonged was not a question that worried him. What use would it have been anyway? This was not a country ruled by ordinary laws. Here, he himself was the only master. The towns and other centers of civilization were far off. Here it was "somewhere"; it was "in the plains." The tax-collector took only as much as the boyar consented to give; military authority never searched for deserters here, nor justice for criminals. No roads touched the estate. There were no churches, and nobody had ever heard of schools. All there was, was land, and more land that had to be worked, and the boyar collected the folk he needed as he could. That was why Mr. George did not waste time in questioning

21

Nita Lepadatu any further. He saw he had to do with a pauper with no family, no village, but seemingly robust and a worker; and this was enough for him.

"Agreed!" he said good-humoredly. "I'll take you on, Nita Lepadatu, to look after the cattle and if you work reasonably well, I will pay you honestly. I'll give you a coat and a fur-lined jacket, boots whenever you need them, and something to cover your head. As for food you won't lack that. Thank God, we have plenty here. You will sleep in some hut or other, with other servants of the estate. . . . And try to behave decently, and I'll reward you accordingly."

"Master," replied Nita in a low voice, "up to now I've never done anything but serve. . . . I hope you will be satisfied with me."

The boyar drew a small notebook out of his pocket and wrote down the name of the new servant. After agreeing exactly on the wage, he put this down along with his other obligations. Then he shut up the notebook and said: "That's all. You can go with the old man now. Tomorrow I will fix the details of your work."

Mr. George pulled a coin out of his pocket and gave it to Nita:

"Be honest," he said, "and work hard and all will go well. Good luck!"

The new servant kissed the boyar's hand and followed the old man who was standing a few paces back. Mr. George shut the veranda door. The men put their hats on again and made their way back towards the huts.

"There, you are staying with us after all," said uncle Nastase gaily.

"I'm glad too," said Nita. "I'd like to buy a drop of brandy and have a drink."

"All right, my lad, very good . . . only there's no pub around here—but look here, on Saturday evening someone usually goes by on horseback and fetches some. We'll drink our healths later on, don't worry, in honor of the moment when we met. I think from now on you'll be living with us. The boyar is a really good man."

"Indeed . . . he's young and friendly," Lepadatu said pensively.

The sun had set, and the autumn twilight was fresh. In the huts, fires were being lit. The sounds of lowing of cattle, barking of dogs, and all sorts of human voices could be heard.

In a sudden silence they heard the noise of galloping horses and shouts which echoed from one hill to another.

Suddenly in the purple sunset a flight of crows rose from somewhere with croaks and cries of alarm, soared up in a compact group, then scattered rapidly in the failing light and disappeared.

Uncle Nastase and Nita Lepadatu approached the huts and could distinctly hear the voices of people returning from work. Above, beyond the cattle-pen at the bottom of the ravine, a number of fires burned brightly. People were stirring the maize porridge; their dark shadows were moving strangely in the light of the flames.

They came up to a fire. They felt the smell of the maize

porridge in their nostrils. Thick steam hovered above a big cauldron in which a mutton stew was simmering. The laborers were waiting for their supper. They were a varied lot, in varied clothes. There were gentle, fair-skinned faces; there were dark ones with shining eyes. You saw white clothes like those you find on the banks of the Moldova; you saw dark ones like those worn by the people of the plains. Some were wearing large felt hats; others, round hats of plaited straw sewn with scarlet thread; others, old fur caps worn out with rains and scorching sun.

Some of the children who happened to be there, urchins of ten to twelve years old, were bareheaded—the only headgear they possessed being a shock of tufted and tangled hair. Several women were coming and going as well, with dark brown kerchiefs and blouses. Their faces were darker and seemed sadder than the men's. All of them were silent, crushed by the day's labor. In the shelter of the wicker fences which surrounded the cattle enclosure the fires burned brightly, lighting up this variegated crowd with its fantastic red flickerings. A thin boy with a long neck every now and then seized armfuls of reeds from a huge pile and fed the fires with them.

Uncle Nastase and Nita Lepadatu crouched on the ground. One of the men servants from the manor house was stirring the maize porridge with a small wooden spoon while another was standing ready with a huge ladle before the mutton stew.

The hungry people were waiting with their bowls. No one seemed to notice the stranger's presence. It was only after the ladlefuls of stew and the large slices were handed

24

round and everybody had begun to eat in silence, that they looked up and around them, through the reddish light of the flames. They noticed the newcomer and began to talk to him.

That evening the stranger had to answer a great many people, though he knew very few of them.

It was only late into the night, when those who had eaten enough went away and only a few stayed on by the rush-fire, that Nita Lepadatu began to know some of the mud-hut dwellers.

He got to know Gheorghe Barba, the oldest herdsman, and Mihalache Prescurie, the boyar's gamekeeper, and old Irimia Izdrail of the barns.

As on every Saturday night, they were sitting by the fire waiting for the boy who had gone off on horseback to fetch the drink.

At length it became calm all around. There was a light at the manor; a few fires were burning in the huts. Here and there voices could be heard. In this Godforsaken part of the world, lapped on every side by an ocean of shadows and stillness, these voices which murmured rather than spoke were somehow soft and friendly.

The boy arrived with the brandy. Sitting around the fire now, the people began to drink together and to discuss the difficulties of the autumn work and preparations for winter.

All at once the sound of a galloping horse pierced the dense air of the night and came nearer; the horse stopped above the cattle-pen.

Uncle Nastase said with a grin: "It's Sandu Faliboga."

"Himself!" exclaimed a rough, hoarse voice.

By the glow of the fires they saw a lean man, long-necked, with shining eyes sunken in two dark hollows beneath his brow.

He had wound his whip around his neck and was laughing. Two of his upper teeth were missing.

"I came along post haste," he said quickly. "From the windmill. . . . If you could just see Mr. Nastratin running after his horses!"

He laughed heartily, and his little eyes twinkled. He looked around and noticed the jug.

"You've got some drink?" he asked in a loud voice. "Pass the mug to me."

After drinking he looked around him again and saw Nita Lepadatu.

"Who's this?" he asked abruptly, throwing back his head.

When he spoke, his Adam's apple slipped up and down under the skin of his neck.

"He's new," replied uncle Nastase with a smile. "He's been taken on for the cattle."

"Ah, good. Where do you come from?"

"From Negoiesti," replied Lepadatu in a soft voice.

"And what's your name?"

"Nita."

"Nita what?"

"Nita Lepadatu."

"Why have you come here?"

"I came to look for work."

"Work? We'll see about that."

He examined the stranger fiercely. He swallowed a second gulp of brandy and cleared his throat noisily.

"This is damned strong! . . . And how did you run away from Negoiesti?"

"I didn't. I left of my own free will."

"So, all right. We'll see about that too! Then, you've been taken on for the beasts. You must know, my lad, that you'll be under my orders. My name is Sandu Faliboga. Have you heard of me?"

"Pleased to meet you, Sandu Faliboga. I've never heard of you."

"Then you will, and from now on you'll know who I am. If you're hard-working, you'll get on pretty well with me; if not, by God . . ."

Faliboga gave a hoarse laugh, lifted his head and went on:

"Ah, if you could only see Mr. Nastratin searching for his horses! I watched him, towards sunset, from the top of a hillock. Mr. Nastratin is not fit to hold a candle to people like us. I'm a cunning one and I know all about horses, like everything else. You might think his herd had nothing to do but to stray on our estate. . . . Our boyar used to find the grass trampled down everywhere and the fields devastated. As for the horses, no trace of them. How to catch anyone and find them, that was the problem, if Nastratin's rascals always managed to lead the horses away before sunrise. 'That's how it is, is it?' says I to myself. . . . You wait and see. So last night I took my white mare and went on to Nastratin's estate, and got near his horses. Well, my mare's bell started tinkling, and slowly, one after the other, all the dear little brutes began to follow me. Now I know my way about, and I know my business. Sometimes I went around that way, sometimes I cut through there, till I had led all the party home to the manor. Now they're all at the manor, and Mr. Nastratin is worrying and fretting. You'll see now what a fine he'll have to pay. Things can't go on that way, men! Before, these beasts roamed the estate from end to end. Now all that's finished, I can tell you! Faliboga has his eye on them. I've a whip and I've a gun. Bailiffs, servants, watchmen, I don't ask who they are. I strike at anyone if I catch him on our estate! I am bound to be faithful. It's nobody's business if we go two or three steps on a neighbor's estate . . . but as for ours, beware of touching it!"

Faliboga stopped and looked about him angrily.

"Where's the mug? My throat's gone dry." He turned to Nita: "You, Lepadatu, are you married?"

"No, I'm not," answered Lepadatu curtly.

"I *am* married, and I've got a she-devil of a wife who rides horseback and shoots like a man."

"Much good may it do you both," said Lepadatu, without looking at his interlocutor.

Faliboga paused with the mug of drink halfway to his lips and frowned. "I say," he exclaimed furiously. "How dare you talk to me like that?"

"Why, I answer as you question," said Nita slowly.

"Oh, it's like that, is it? You are forgetting perhaps that you'll have to work with me?"

"No, I'm not forgetting anything."

"And you aren't afraid of me?"

"I'm not . . ."

Faliboga leaped to his feet and seized his whip. But Lepadatu had sprung from his place, quickly drawing from his cloak an impressive brass club with a dogwood handle.

"Listen, Faliboga," said Lepadatu. "I am a peaceful man. With a single word, with the smallest kindness you can do anything you like with me. But don't you try to cross me, for no good will come of it. And you might as well know that I'm not to be frightened."

Faliboga had lowered his head and was staring at Nita. Firmly, without blinking, Lepadatu returned his stare.

"Come, come," suddenly intervened Uncle Nastase Tentea in his thin voice. "What the devil, men! You've no sooner set eyes on each other and you're fighting like cat and dog."

"Uncle Nastase," said Nita placidly, putting back the club into his cloak. "You've said just the right word. I have nothing against anybody and I'm always glad to be everybody's friend. There's no hatred in my heart."

"You, my friend!" cried Faliboga, in a fury. Then he burst out laughing, showing bad teeth.

"Hey, Nita," he went on, "Your club is a beauty, you know. With such a pal you could travel the wide world without fear. Come on, I'll clink glasses with you all the same! Only you're going to obey me all the same: you're still young, and as for me, my hair is grey."

"That's good! It shall be as you wish," Lepadatu answered, taking the mug Faliboga offered him.

Sandu Faliboga crouched near the fire. He rolled a cigarette, lit it, then sprang up again.

"I'm going to take a turn as far as the Wolf's Valley and

come right back," he announced in his hoarse voice. He cracked his whip and went out puffing at his cigarette. They heard the sound of the white mare galloping off, first close, then gradually farther and farther off, till it was lost in the silence of the night.

Those left around the fire kept silent for quite a while. Uncle Nastase threw a new armful of rushes into the flames. Gheorghe Barba brought the jug of brandy into the light. Now the huts were plunged in complete darkness. Alone, in the darkness above, the stars were sparkling. The wind which had blown all day still shivered lightly in the wattles of the cattle-pen.

It was Mihalache Prescurie, the keeper, who broke the silence:

"The boyar has never had a bailiff like Faliboga before, and will never have another like him. He goes over the estate like the wind, you might say. These fields have never been watched as they are now."

"Where does he come from?" asked Lepadatu.

Prescurie turned to him.

"I don't know," he answered. "Nobody knows. But they all know when it was he came here. It was in summer, and a stranger was found sleeping near a haystack. We heard about it at once, and in the evening we took him in beside the fire and gave him something to eat. He told us that he came from a long way off, that he was being hunted by the mounted police. But where he came from, really, only God knew. . . . Perhaps he had escaped from somewhere, from the galleys, maybe. The boyar soon heard there was a stranger about on his land. He even saw him on the top of the haycock, hiding in the maize, but he left him in peace. Why, has anyone ever seen gendarmes around here? And then a fugitive, if he isn't left in peace takes offense and may set the corn on fire or pounce upon you. So, one evening the boyar came to have a look at the cattle-pen and he met the man. He said a friendly word to him and took him into his service. Since then Faliboga has stayed here with us. So, now the boyar has a hard-working, tireless and merciless servant in him."

"Indeed, he seems to be as hardworking as he is cruel," Nita Lepadatu put in.

Uncle Irimia Izdrail, the oldest of them all, pensively eyed the newcomer.

"But you, my lad," he said, "where you were you had a lot to bear. . . . You know, when I see a man, I read his thoughts and see if he has suffered a lot."

"Who can say he has not suffered?" asked Nita. "I can't remember my parents. I grew up among strangers: some of them beat me; others were kind and sorry for me. That's how I learned to prize people who have good hearts. It's as if God had given them a special gift. I've always worked; I've always been somebody's servant. And I can say truly, I've always been an honest and faithful servant. I've travelled along the banks of the Prut and the bank of the Jijia. I've heard tell that beyond that there were other countries with big villages, large towns and many people, but I never went to see them. I've liked it better over in these parts where people are fewer! I could never have gone farther afield, I was so poor. On my side I always worked as well as I could, but the boyars didn't give me much in exchange. It's just that I'm not very lucky. I've lived in huts like these; I've eaten what they put on my plate. I've worked harder than a beast of burden, and I never picked a quarrel with anyone. One fine day I said to myself: 'Look here, it's time for me to roam around the world a bit too.' For the present, I've stopped here . . . and it seems to me already as if I didn't want to move off again. . . . What could I do in a big town where there are lots of people? It strikes me I'd be better off with the animals; it's with them that I grew up, and it's with them that I get on best. . . ."

"Ah, my boy!" said Uncle Irimia Izdrail, "truly it can be seen that you've had much to put up with. All the same, let me tell you it is a pity not to see a lot of people and the marvels of the towns. At least when one is young. Myself, I've heard from one and another that now there are sorts of big fire-spitting carts. And that they build houses three and even four stories high. And that in those towns people swarm about night and day, like they do here during the fair at Saveni. But I don't need to know all that, because I'm old already. Look you, Nita, we have gathered here, round a pot of brandy; now you, you come from the plain; Mihalache Prescurie is from beyond the Prut; Gheorghe Barba, he came down the mountain to these parts at the time when he was a child; and all the folk who live on this estate now, and labor on it, strangers from everywhere, all of us have settled down in this desert because we found a little more land, a little more space here. . . . Take myself, you see me, a poor old man. Tomorrow, or after tomorrow, who knows, I shall go. . . . God made me settle here too—for such is his power . . . and you, my boy, must know that I was a Jew in my youth and that God one day, seventy years ago, inspired me to be a convert. And now I am a Moldavian and a Christian and I live with you others, according to the will of God on this corner of the earth."

"Now look at me, brother Irimia," said uncle Nastase Tentea in his shrill, bleating voice; "where did I come from? Hm . . . well, well! I too came from a long way off to settle here. . . . And it is twelve or thirteen years already now since my wife left me and went away, leaving me alone with my daughter Marghiolita. Hm . . . well, well! It's Saturday night and we are having a drink and a chat. . . . How many years have we been meeting here every Saturday ? . . . Now, this lad Nita is young, but one day he will be like us, and when he drinks with the other men he will remember us, the old men of today. This is the way we pass the time, always among ourselves—for we have neither priest nor church. We are poor folks living in a lonely way. . . ."

Gheorghe Barba began to laugh, shaking his hoary head:

"This is the way that this Jew has been talking as far back as I can remember, young man . . . and old Nastase who bleats more than he talks. Say one thing, say another but always the same thing. And once we have clinked and drunk our pots of brandy, we go off to bed and to sleep. I am from the mountains and there are forests over there. Have you others seen forests like ours? If you laid ten estates as big as our boyar's end to end—what am I saying? a hundred estates—they would not reach as far as our forest, our fine, green fir-trees forest. And you should see the torrents which rush down from these forests, and hear them roar . . . as the wind roars here in winter. Ah, out there it's another world. And who knows, I might go back there one day. . . . Bah! the times I've said that, and yet I've grown old as our master's herdsman and never been back to the places where I lived in my youth. I'd like to go there, even if it's only to die there."

For a long time Nita Lepadatu listened to these men talking round the fire. From time to time his turn came to take the pot of brandy and swallow a few mouthfuls of the liquid flame. Gradually, as he drank, a soft languor came over him, a feeling of deeper and deeper tenderness. After a time the sound of voices talking faded, became very faint and finished by mingling with the light whisper of the autumn wind which slid along the wattle fencing of the cattle-pen.

The very next morning, on a Sunday, Nita Lepadatu began his work with the boyar's cattle. Sandu Faliboga led him to the various pens, and, in his rough voice, taught him what he was to do:

"Here are the beasts we look after, my lad. In this pen are the milk cows; there, the barren ones; farther on, the heifers. As you see, all the beasts are properly arranged. You'll be in charge of the milk cows. You'll have to take them to graze in the best places, near the marshes where the grass is still green, where there are still a few tufts of millet left."

"All right, we'll go, and you will show me the places too."

"We'll go; though even these ragamuffins know them."

Then, addressing the latter, he added: "Hey, you there! I've brought you someone! You will obey him or look out for your ears! Off we go now!" he shouted.

The boys drew the bolts of the pen, and the beasts began to come out through it, one after the other. There were little ones, roans, red and white, thin and fat. The boys ran around, whistling and shouting, cracking their whips and striving to push the herd towards the pond.

A big cloud of black dust soon rose in waves sweeping down on all sides.

"For the present, my lad," said Faliboga, "you will take this little gray horse. You will find a stick, a bundle of rope and a whip hanging from the pommel of the saddle. Do your best with these lads to guard the master's wealth and don't let it be wasted. . . ."

They both got into their saddles and followed the herd. Faliboga gave him instructions and advice in his unfriendly voice. After a short time he said looking frowningly at the young man: "Well, Nita. You nearly caught it from me last night."

"But why?"

"Just like that . . . don't ask me why. I don't like anyone defying me."

"I never offended you, not I. It was you who looked at me in such a queer sort of way."

35

"I looked at you in a queer sort of way?" cried Faliboga, looking hard into Nita's eyes.

"Yes, you did look at me in a queer sort of way. I can't help it."

"Listen, young man!" said the bailiff slowly and hoarsely. "I'm going to give you a piece of good advice. You must behave toward me—do you know how? as with a glass of fine crystal. . . ."

With a prompt movement Faliboga turned his white mare around.

"And pay attention to the beasts!" he cried again. "Good-bye."

He cracked his whip and rode away hell-bent for leather, disappearing in a thick cloud of dust.

The road led towards the pond. The herd descended slowly; at the head of it a few cowbells tinkled. The sun peeped through copper-colored clouds. Suddenly the air was suffused with a gilded red glow. Then, the faint light flooded over hills and valleys. The manor and the huts were left far behind; the lake, over which flights of wild ducks were flying, was passed too. After some time the bells were no longer heard. The beasts stopped, stretched out their necks and began peacefully to graze the damp grass of a marshy valley.

Seated on his little gray horse, Nita Lepadatu went around the herd. The boys, when he passed near them, threw him furtive glances. Sometimes, as a cow strayed from the herd, a cry rose in the fresh morning air: "Hooee! This way! Come back!"

But all sound of voices was swiftly extinguished, and

silence began to cover everything. At irregular intervals a little bell sounded. The cows advanced slowly grazing the fresh grass.

From time to time a bird crossed the sky above the valley, leaving only the trace of a shrill cry. Whence did it come? Why was it straying in this solitude?

Lepadatu jumped down and tied his horse to a stake. Then he tried to get into conversation with the boys. He inquired the name and habits of each cow, and the boys took him from one to the other, answering all his questions. A little later he asked them their own names, and about their parents. The father and mother of some of them lived in the huts; others were poor orphans who had strayed here from some distant village in search of a bit of bread.

Nita Lepadatu questioned them gently and, listening to their voices, thought of the new country to which he had himself wandered and of the life which the future held in store for him.

NOVEMBER had passed, bringing change in the droughty weather. Nita with his herd had explored every corner and the farthest recesses of the estate. Now he knew the paths, the springs, the marshes and lakes like his hand. He knew, equally well, the names of the people and of the beasts, Faliboga's outbursts of temper, and the boyar's tastes. He went from time to time to the little mill down in a valley, hollowed out by a stream, to have some oats ground, and in the evening, with the help of his boys and some of the men from the huts, he prepared a kind of malt which he added to the meager autumn feed of the cows.

Otherwise, and for the time being at least, life was easy.

But Nita was well aware that soon the autumn rains would come, then the first frosts, and finally winter, with its terrible snowstorms. Then life would become harder, out-of-doors in all weather with the beasts, or behind the wattle fences of the enclosures, or under some thatched roof.

Coming and going with his herd, he saw the people working at the huts: they blocked up holes; they mended rotten roofs.

The boyar never left them, ceaselessly gave them advice and showed them what they ought to do.

This young master, as far as Nita could gather, personally directed all the business of his estate. He rose at dawn, roamed here and there, never resting till nightfall, in his light carriage drawn by two little horses; scrambled up hills, climbed down slopes, inspected the ploughing, then the sheep-pens, went to the stables and to the barns; he asked endless questions, told off those with whom he found fault, grew angry, calmed down— and went off as fast as he had come, in his little carriage; one could read on his swarthy face and in his bright eyes a great desire and unshakable resolve to work as much as his strength would let him, and to make a fortune.

"It's just as uncle Nastase said," thought Nita; "why does he need so much money and so much land?"

One Saturday afternoon of this calm November, Nita Lepadatu decided to go and visit the old man's hut. He had not been there since the day of his arrival, having, as a matter of fact, not had one minute's respite.

The old man was at the winnower's shed. The white dog began to bark furiously, trying to hurl itself at Nita's legs. Uncle Nastase came out at once, a stick in hand, and curses on his lips.

"The devil take you! Coltun! Get down I say!" Its head

down, and growling, the dog retreated behind the shed.

The young man was able to approach and the old peasant, recognizing him, smiled.

"Hm . . . well, well!" he cried in his shrill voice. "It must be a month since you came here last . . . since the day when a good wind blew you to these parts. How goes it, Nita?"

"Very well," replied Lepadatu, putting down his polished cudgel and arranging his hooded cloak.

"So how are you getting on with Faliboga?"

"All right!"

The old man began to laugh.

"Hm . . . well, well! ha-ha-ha! Hm . . . well, well! I could see very well, that I could, that he wanted to make you dance to his tune. Bah! there's nothing to worry about. It's the work that does it . . . you have to do with all sorts of folk."

"I mind my own business, and we get on all right," said Nita, giving a look around. "But you, uncle Nastase, are you still winnowing this corn? It seems to run like a river, it never ends. . . ."

"Aye, that's how it is on our land," said the old man proudly. "The year's been good. We've loaded I don't know how many carts already and there are as many again and more. I wonder how much money the boyar has got? A deal, a great deal. I wanted to find out one day, but the master was a bit put out because of this drought. And I left it."

"Drought is a bad thing for ploughmen," remarked Nita.

40

"It's a bad thing for everybody, lad. But, what can be done about it? I even said so to the boyar: 'Mr. George,' I said, 'there's nothing we can do about it. It's God that sends us all that. When he wants it we shall have rain.'"

"And what did he answer? Did he laugh?"

"No, he didn't laugh. He shook his head and went in to the manor house worriedly. That's how it is. He may be a boyar but he can't pretend to have any less worry. Hm . . . well well! come along now to the hut," the old man added, inviting him with a nod.

They edged along between the barns. The ground was strewn with heaps of chaff and maize husks. As they gradually moved away, the noise of the wind and the growling of the winnowing faded. Nita looked up and perceived, for the fraction of a second, Marghiolita's head framed in the door of the hut.

"Hey, little one!" cried the old man when they were near enough. Uncle Nastase gave a little laugh. "Hey, Marghiolita, can't you hear? Go and get some fresh water. Perhaps you've got a bit of sugar too? Look, he's come back, that thirsty chap."

Lepadatu smiled when the girl hurried out of the hut, with the bucket in her left hand and the cup in her right.

"Now," he said, "I'm not so tired nor thirsty as I was that day . . ." And looking her straight in the eyes, he added: "How goes it?"

"How do you think it goes?" replied Marghiolita. "Always alone and always working."

"You've been up to the manor too," the old man put in. "The nun has taught her to make lace. She gave her some

41

sugar too. Offer him some, Marghiolita, offer him some sugar and some water as the boyars do."

With an embarrassed smile the girl pulled a crumpled piece of paper out of her blouse. She slowly unfolded it and chose several lumps of sugar. She gave some to Nita and to her father as well, then put the bucket of water and the little mug between them.

The lad sat down in front of the hut; the old man dropped on to a sheaf of maize stalks. Marghiolita was standing, and Nita Lepadatu, biting his sugar, noticed that she was wearing a white blouse with lace at the sleeves and at the collar, that her hair was shining and well brushed, and that her thick plaits were twisted in a crown around her head. She seemed to him taller than the first time, and her waist better held in by her red belt.

He looked up at her face, tanned by the summer sun; she avoided his gaze, fixing her hazel eyes on something else.

"This sugar smells of basil," said Nita, filling the mug with water.

The girl gave a short burst of laughter. Her eyes narrowed and sparkled.

"Hm . . . well, well!" said uncle Tentea. "These girls, see, they've got a habit of putting all sorts of weeds into their bosoms."

"But, father, basil isn't a weed!" answered Marghiolita quickly.

She took the bucket and the mug and hurried back into the hut. The two men heard her bustling about and moving things for quite a time while they sat chatting

42

in the soft rays of the sun. But when she no longer heard the old man's shrill voice, she came out and sat down not far from Nita, modestly and timidly as befits a young girl. Uncle Tentea had risen and gone to see some young pigs squeaking in their sty. When Nita saw he was far enough off, he turned to Marghiolita with a friendly smile:

"It was yesterday that I thought of coming up to the barns," he said. "And see, I've been lucky with the fine weather."

"Yes, we're having a beautiful autumn," replied Marghiolita. "I've even got some flowers which are going to bloom."

"Where do you get flowers from? You don't see many hereabouts."

"It was the housekeeper at the manor house who gave me two roots this summer. She has some. She taught me how to plant them, near the hut, where they will get plenty of sun in a bed of dung. They grew, and they are beautiful now. They are going to bloom soon."

Their eyes met a moment and they smiled.

"Where I come from, you don't see flowers outside our huts," said Nita. "The miller down there told me that in other places there are big gardens with trees and lots of flowers. He's a German and has roamed about the world. He knows so many things! He told me once that he had been to several big towns, so big that two whole days were not enough to cross them. He talked about mills too, with motors that go by fire, like our boyar has for the threshing machine—very big mills, which could grind the harvest of a whole country. He talked about trains. . . ."

"What are those?" asked Marghiolita in surprise.

"I don't know, but I've heard it said they are similar to carts that go with motors; even if it's raining or snowing —and terribly fast. One moment they are there and the next you can't see them."

"What marvels," murmured the girl. "Like in a fairytale. . . . Down here we've nothing like all that."

"The miller has a watch too," added Nita.

"So has our boyar," interrupted Marghiolita. "The housekeeper let me see it . . ."

"I should like to roam about the world and see all these things," said Nita with a smile.

Marghiolita was pensive and said nothing.

That autumn afternoon was very calm and an infinite silence seemed to sadden the wide stretches of land.

All noises had ceased. Long spider webs shone in the nearby heath. Sometimes a scarcely perceptible breeze lifted the long, silvery, silken threads, making them whirl in the still air. Nita and the girl were left alone, sitting near each other before the door of the hut. They had stopped talking, but something mysterious seemed to draw them near one another. All at once a weasel emerged from a small elder bush near a dung-hill. It stopped, fearful in the radiant daylight, and began looking around with its little black eyes, like pinheads. Its fur was so white that it looked like the faint blue of the purest snow. It soon vanished like a dart. The two young people turned to each other and smiled—both with the same tender smile.

At sunset; with this feeling of budding love in his heart, Nita Lepadatu went back to his beasts. He inspected their pens, carried them their rations of oatmeal with the help of his boys, and the women brought their buckets to milk the cows. In the huts they were lighting lamps and fires. Then silence settled, little by little, and above, the dark blue sky hung like a canopy, studded with large golden nails.

Rolled up in his sheepskin jacket, Nita Lepadatu lay on his back near his beasts, on a heap of straw. He looked at the sky. He counted the stars and softly murmured the names of the biggest, which he had learned from the old men among whom he had spent his childhood. At first he thought of nothing in particular. He enjoyed being alone. Then, after a few moments, he seemed to see Marghiolita's eyes shining near him in the darkness. He closed his eyelids and it was as if a dream had brought her beside him. He understood then that he was fond of her and that he longed to see her again.

He reopened his burning eyes quickly and saw the immensity of the sky and the twinkling of the stars; he looked all around and listened. Nothing could be heard but the beasts, quiet in their pens, chewing the cud. The boyar's house and the huts were buried in silence.

Nita stood up and pulled his buckled belt tighter. He pushed the brass-headed cudgel into his cloak, threw his sheepskin jacket over his shoulder and set off towards the barns.

A single fire was still burning near the cattlepen, not far from the huts where the old people lived. He advanced towards it and, when within a few feet of it, he clearly distinguished Faliboga's rough voice and uncle Nastase's thin bleat. He no longer hesitated but started immediately uphill. He did not slow down before he saw the bulk of the barns in the darkness. He went around them carefully in order to get to the door. But the big white dog heard him and started barking furiously. It jumped out and hurled itself forward as if it wanted to knock him down.

"Coltun . . . hey, Coltun!" the lad called out coaxingly.

But it was useless trying to quiet the brute. Defending himself as best as he could with his stick, the young man advanced step by step towards the hut.

A thick, very sleepy voice called from the winnower's shed:

"Who's there?"

At the same time, Marghiolita's clear voice echoed through the night, calling the dog. Coltun stopped barking immediately, the winnower's shed relapsed into silence, and Nita stole rapidly towards the hut.

"Is that you?" asked the girl.

Nita did not reply. He went up to her, stopped before her and seized her hands.

"I thought at once who it might be," said the girl again. "Why did you come?"

"I just thought . . . I thought I'd come and see you," answered Nita in a voice choked with emotion.

Marghiolita let him take her by the waist, and Nita, pressing her against him noticed the scent of basil in her bosom.

"No," she said suddenly in a low voice. "Come here during the day and we'll talk. Go away now. Father will be coming back."

Nita had not thought she would slip from his arms so easily. He only realized it when she had escaped. He heard the hut door close and the bolt creak. The dog began barking again, more furiously than before.

"Who goes there?" shouted the sleepy voice from the shed once more.

Nita took the path by which he had come, and went downhill.

"The girl's a she-devil," he thought. "She knows how to talk and behave at night. . . . I believe I heard her laugh after she had shut the door. . . . As far as I can see, the first thing to do is to make friends with the dog. . . . As for her, it seems that she doesn't dislike me. Ah, she knew I'd be in a hurry to come back. . . ."

He was talking to himself in a low voice and smiling as he approached the pens.

"It's love, it's love," he thought joyfully, and something indefinable trembled through his whole being.

Without exactly knowing what he was doing, he returned to his place near the beasts, on to his heap of hay. He gazed at the stars again and did not even feel the cool air of the night sweeping lightly over his burning forehead.

A few days later there were violent downpours, at intervals, then the long, the endless rains of autumn set in, like compact layers of mist. High gray walls blotted the horizon out on every side. A cold, steady drizzle fell from a low ceiling of clouds, soaking the buildings, the beasts' shelters, the deserted pens. The rich soil absorbed the water through all its cracks, then disgorged it, so that in the courtyards and on the roads, men and beasts paddled in an appalling swamp. For a whole week the people of the huts toiled to complete the cattle shelters. Now they began to carry forage into the pens, while the beasts stayed there, gloomy and downcast, head to head, hardly stirring behind the palings under the thatched roofs. They only nibbled at their fodder and all around a cold moisture permeated everything.

The people did not leave their huts. They mainly stayed before the hearth, where the fire burned constantly, trying to dry their damp rags. From time to time they came out, putting a piece of sacking on their heads, slithering about with their pigskin sandals all worn, and falling down in the mud, then went indoors again as quickly as possible.

In such weather Faliboga was more active than ever. On his white mare, his head and shoulders covered with a hood, he was everywhere at once and forcibly drove the people to their work. The boyar, who was always bored by such weather, had nothing more to do in his house. He had sold his corn and the pigs that he had fattened during the summer. His accounts were already made up for the year. So, one fine day he said good-bye to the nun and his bookkeeper, left Faliboga and the servants, ordered his carriage and went away to a life of pleasure. After his departure, heavier rains poured down from the sky. And Faliboga, gazing at the drowned fields, said with satisfaction:

"Our master is lucky! Indeed, he is!"

Nothing in the daily routine of the estate changed with the master's absence. Barns and shed were overflowing with food, clothing, and all that was needed for all the servants. As for Faliboga, a faithful and watchful attendant, he was as savage as a bloodhound.

During the gloomy and desolate days, plodding through the rain, Nita Lepadatu had little time to nurse his lovesickness. He went a second time to the barns. The hut was falling in under the weight of the damp, and its one small room was gloomy and cold.

Marghiolita smiled sweetly at him, but the light which pierced the window-pane seemed to cast a grayish shadow on her face. At first he chatted easily with her and the old man; but after a time, towards evening, all three became silent, having no more to say to one another. The melancholy of the dusk invaded the hut, while the rain continued to tap lightly on the flat roof of beaten earth.

Lepadatu came out of the hut with his heart full of great longing for the spring. From the threshold, Marghiolita's eyes followed him for a while.

He put his hood over his fur cap and went off, slipping every step. Wrapped in his thoughts, he slowly descended from the barns towards the cattle-pens.

Suddenly he remembered the autumn day when he had realized for the first time that he was in love. A heavy sadness came over him, and his heart filled with a deep feeling of discontent. Ah, yes! winter is indeed hard for

49

poor folk who have to live like moles under the earth.

As he approached the pen he caught sight of Faliboga on horseback in the driving rain, waiting for him.

"What does that fellow want now?" growled Nita between his teeth, pulling his hood over his eyes.

He wanted to pass by the bailiff, but the latter stopped him in his rough, hoarse voice:

"Not so fast, my lad, not so fast. Where are you off to?"

Nita felt the mare's muzzle near his elbow. Faliboga in his gray-hooded cloak dismounted quickly and came near the young man.

"Where have you been?" he asked curtly, seizing his arm.

"Leave me alone!" retorted Nita, annoyed. "What do you want? Don't you think I've worries enough as it is?"

"How is it that you left the beasts and went off?"

"If I left them it was because I had seen after them before going."

"Ha, my lad! I've had a bone to pick with you for a long time. See, you've met me at a moment when I'm in a good mood."

"Uncle Sandu, I see you've had something against me from the beginning . . . but I can't do anything about it. I mind my own business, so you mind yours."

Nita had spoken firmly. He wanted to go off to the sheds, but Faliboga bounded forward, caught him up and seized his arm again, forcing him to turn around where he stood.

"Stop a minute! What's the hurry?" he cried harshly.

With a rapid movement Nita disengaged himself.

"Uncle Sandu," he shouted drily, "what do you want?"

"Look here," shouted Faliboga, his eyes popping out of his head. "*I* am the master here, and you must take care how you speak to me! Could you explain why there is so much rain that I'm sick of it? And so much mud that you drown in it? And why I have so many worries that I don't know where to turn? I've got to let off steam, my lad, and crack someone over the head with my whip, and, you see, I've decided to whip you, Nita Lepadatu."

Faliboga was grinning. Nita frowned and, throwing his hood back over his shoulders, took two steps backwards.

"Aren't you pleased?" brayed Faliboga. "Wait a moment. I want to show you how to learn to love my whip."

He dropped his mare's bridle, took two steps back in his turn and shook loose his black whip.

"If you dare stand up to me," he roared again, "I'll split you in half like a chicken! My lad, I did a good few things in my youth. I want you to fear me as all the others do . . . to tremble when you hear the name of Faliboga!"

"But what on earth have I done to you, uncle Sandu?" exclaimed Nita puzzled.

Faliboga brandished his whip. But like a spring uncoiling, Lepadatu sprang on him and, grasping his right arm, twisted it and bent it behind his back.

He seized the struggling left arm as well, and pulled it down to the other—with the whip he tied the bailiff's wrists. Then, panting with rage, he threw him on to the ground, sat down heavily on him and drew out his brass cudgel.

Faliboga breathed heavily and rolled his eyes fero-

51

ciously; between two snorts he cursed with hatred and his breath stank of brandy.

"What do you want?" cried Nita with dim eyes, bending over him.

Drops of rain sparkled on the polished brass of the cudgel.

"Nita, my lad," groaned Faliboga suddenly with fright. "Don't kill me!"

Lepadatu leaped to his feet. He thrust his cudgel into his belt, behind his back, and, his expression suddenly softening, he helped the bailiff to his feet.

"I don't want to kill you, uncle Sandu," he hastened to say. "I've got nothing against you . . . I'd rather leave this place, win my bread as I can, than have trouble with you all the time, and perhaps commit God knows what crime! Here's your whip, and your hood too. Cover your head; it's raining. Get on your mare and go back to the huts. As for me, you won't see me any more."

"What are you saying?" Faliboga burst out, livid in the face. "Why didn't you hit me with your cudgel? I thought you had not got it on you. I thought you would have left it at home before going to see Nastase's daughter."

"Uncle Sandu, leave me alone. I've not got your heart."

He pulled his hood down over his eyes and waited a while, not knowing whether he should go towards the sheds or whether to take the road to some new, unknown horizon.

Faliboga looked at him steadily as if he expected a word or gesture. He seized Nita by the arm again, forcing him to turn around.

52

"Listen Nita," he said in an even hoarser voice. "Don't go away; I want us to make it up."

Nita watched him, a slight smile on his lips.

"Why are you laughing?" cried Faliboga. "You don't trust me! Oh, I was a terrible man in my youth, you know. I somehow had something against you and I've irritated you. But I see you have your own troubles . . . so I want us to make it up. . . ."

"Let's drop it," said Nita, annoyed. He turned to go.

"Don't anger me, my lad," barked Faliboga. "I want us to make it up and have a drink."

Holding on tight to Nita's right arm, the bailiff strove to drag him off.

"Come with me!"

Lepadatu followed him in silence. The rain was still falling, fine and fast, drowning the dusk in its mist.

Nobody had seen or heard what had passed between the two men.

The inhabitants of the huts had all gone to their dens. Here and there a faint beam of light flickered and pierced the screen of dampness.

Faliboga and Nita trudged across the broken ground.

Her head down, the mare followed their steps.

They stopped at a hut near the deserted cattlepen, where the old mud-hut dwellers usually gathered on Saturday evenings. This was a Saturday evening; there was light in the hut and, in the warmth, Gheorghe Barba, the herdsman, Irimia Izdrail and Mihalache Prescurie were finishing their supper. Two boys were drying their

53

wet clothes before the wide hearth where bundles of rushes were burning.

Faliboga opened the door with a kick and went inside the hut with Nita Lepadatu at his heels.

"Hey, Grecusor!" he said roughly to a thin and frail boy. "Take my mare on the outside and lead her home. At the same time, tell Jana to come here and bring the jug of wine. And be quick about it. Don't dawdle!"

Grecusor got up from his place like a shadow and went out.

"Say, you others!" cried Faliboga in his broken voice, baring his bad teeth. "I want to stand this lad a treat."

He tapped Nita on the back.

"We had a tiff," he went on, "but now we have made it up! Haven't we, Lepadatu?"

Nita said nothing.

"Aren't you going to say anything, man?" shouted Faliboga in anger. "Ah, you don't know me yet. You don't know how terrible I am . . . just like a vicious dog, my lad. . . . You need only know I don't bite on the sly. Sit down there, Nita, on the bench, near the fire, and take your hood off your head!"

Sandu, the bailiff, pulled off Lepadatu's white cloak, took off his own gray one, forced the lad to sit down on the bench and himself fell on to a low stool before the hearth.

"What's the news, uncle Izdrail?" he began again, with a laugh. "Bless me, I am sick of so much rain. I feel as if I were in a thick fog and stifling there. Here in the hut it's better. How I'd like a bit of booze this evening. . . ."

Uncle Irimia Izdrail replied with a smile: "The rain's

54

sent us by God and we can't do anything about it. As to your idea of a drink, you'll have it if you like."

"Yes, yes . . . I'm going to enjoy myself presently . . . but I'd like to wake up this lad a bit. . . . You aren't saying much, Nita."

"What should I say? I'm listening to you others talking."

"I say! I see you're rather suspicious . . . but it's nothing."

He breathed noisily as though he had a load on his chest, and looked about him.

"Uncle Barba, take your flute and wet it a bit. Then you can play for me as only you know."

"Willingly. Why not?" answered Gheorghe Barba in a thick voice from the corner where he was sitting. They were silent for a while.

Faliboga seemed to be studying the earthen floor. Suddenly he lifted his head and fixed his shining eyes on the door.

"Are you there, Jana?" he asked in a powerful voice.

The door opened and a woman entered, squat and sturdy, with a highly colored face and thick eyebrows. She took off the sack that had protected her from the rain, looked at the gathering and laughed; then, her fists on her hips, she turned to Faliboga.

"What's up, that you have to shout like that?" she shouted, in a man's voice. "Here I am. I've come and brought the jug too."

Grecusor came in carrying the jug and Faliboga hastened to pour the wine into the earthen mugs, inviting the others to help themselves.

"It's a long time since we've seen wine in these parts!"

he said gaily. "At least this is some of the old stuff. . . . I got it in Saveni. . . . Look, I lift my mug and I drink to Jana, for we've been fond of each other for a long time and she has followed me all over the world. And I drink to the health of Nita Lepadatu, so that he can know my heart. . . . Well, uncle Barba, have you got the flute ready?"

He drank off his mug in one gulp and handed it to Jana.

The others clinked in their turn. Lepadatu drank too, Faliboga watching him closely. Gheorghe Barba began to play a tune from his native mountains.

"At home, in the mountains, you'd say the flute had quite a different sound," he said as he finished. "When you play up there, the gorges and the valleys seem to answer back."

"What are you saying, Barba?" shouted Sandu, the bailiff. "Ask Jana, let her tell you what she thinks about it . . . from the time when we used to wander about the mountains."

"Yes, we have seen quite a few places in the world," replied Jana dreamily, coming nearer the cozy warmth of the fire.

'It's true," Faliboga went on. "When I think of the forests and plains we've covered on horseback. . . . Ah, it's that we were doing dangerous work at that time."

The bailiff smiled, agreeably moved by his recollections.

The mugs were filled again and everybody drank. In the light of the flames which flickered in the hearth, Faliboga's eyes glittered violently. Mug in hand, he straightened himself and began to sing hoarsely:

Hey, Jana, Jana, Jana here—
Go and make my bed, my dear,
Where three or four roads cross,
Near a cellar's mouth, on the moss,
I shall hear the taps go
And the good red wine will flow.

"Do you remember, Jana?" he said, his face gleaming strangely. "That's what I sang to you when I asked you to follow me and roam the world with me. And you, how you tortured me, Jana! My heart was black as soot with so much love and sorrow. . . . And that Ilie Ragazan who sang the song I had made for you—and me looking at you, while you looked away . . .

"The lovely girl I loved so,
Loved both tenderly and true . . .
To drown my heavy load of woe
To drink deep was the best thing to do!
And I drank for one day, two days,
And I drank for forty days . . .

. . .

"And I drank away the price of my gray horse so fine,
Without ever feeling the taste of the good wine . . ."

Faliboga kept his eyes on his wife. His voice was harsh; he drawled the words rather than sang them.

He swallowed another mug of wine greedily, then turned to Nita Lepadatu.

"Ah, Nita, my friend! Do you see this woman? It's with her that I went thieving when I was young. If you only knew what rivers we crossed, what forests we roamed, what desert lands we wandered through. . . . Ah, I've forgotten them all! We've been in Dobrogea, and in the Baragan, and beyond the Prut. And we climbed mountains, and then we dropped into the valleys. No one could say the number of horses we stole and transformed into famous breeds . . . I was even shut up for it . . . and I escaped. And Jana looked for me everywhere and always found me. And now, good people, you see I've become an honest and faithful servant. But you still don't know who I am. Sometimes I feel a craving in my heart and I long to go off again. Then I look at my Jana and I have a drink. And Jana's eyes say to me 'Come on!' Only I feel my bones go heavy in my body, and they whisper to me 'stay here!'

> "Ah, there's no thinking
> And ah, there's no knowing
> If there's any ending
> To my desire so glowing . . .

"Go on, Barba, play me something else. . . . My heart's heavy . . . and I see Jana's eyes again saying 'Come on!'"

The woman smiled, illuminated by the flames in the hearth. Her face still retained some traces of beauty, and passions still shone in her eyes. She looked at her man, and a whole past seemed to revive in her memory—a past of folly and wild impulses.

Gheorghe Barba's flute sounded once more in the hut,

but so sadly, with such languor that it might have been, suddenly, the wide plains of the Prut unfolding there, under a bluish autumn light, and that the enchanted song of the infinite was floating everywhere.

Jana wiped a tear with the back of her hand; then, her eyes distant, intoxicated by the wine, she burst out laughing.

"Hey, Nita," said Faliboga after a few minutes, in a thick voice. "Come and drink another mug with me. You are a strong man. . . . You seem to have come from those parts where there are many churches and popes. Your heart's different. You know what pity and friendliness mean . . . as I never knew."

It was late when they left the warmth of the hut to plunge into the black autumn night. The old men went off to their beds. Alone, Gheorghe Barba, wrapping himself in his cloak, decided to take a turn to see how it was going with the boyar's oxen and with the boys who slept beside them.

Nita Lepadatu walked beside Faliboga; Jana was ahead of them.

"Jana," said the bailiff, "go home and get to bed. I'll take my mare and go the rounds. . . . It won't take long."

The woman vanished in the dark. Faliboga fetched his mare.

"Nita, my boy," he said. "Go and get your horse and come with me."

They went down to the cow-pen and Nita brought out his horse. They went off together in the rain, which, cold and pitiless, did not abate for an instant.

They trotted along beside one another for a long time.

Nita hardly recognized the places they were passing. But the bailiff, as if in broad daylight, did not make the slightest mistake in guiding his horse.

"I had a drop too much tonight," he said after a while . . . "but I still know my way about the estate."

They inspected all the pens. Then they went along the pond, passed near the mill, climbed to the sheep pens, and from there went up to the very boundaries on the north side of the estate. As they passed by isolated huts, the dogs growled, lying in the rain. Apart from this, the fields were naked and deserted, and the two men seemed to advance into a black wall which receded gradually as they went forward.

On the way back, Faliboga muttered: "This is the right weather; I know it, I do. . . . Two or three fellows might come and lead off the best beasts, if they aren't being properly guarded."

Going back by the barns and sheds, he called out in his rough voice, and the men on guard answered him sleepily.

The dogs, as sleepy as their masters, merely yelped once or twice, then they were overcome by the shadows of the soaking night.

They stopped much later in front of the manor.

"The nun's asleep too," whispered Faliboga, "alone in the master's house. . . . The bookkeeper is old and goes to bed early with his night-cap pulled over his ears. If there were a fire or if floods invaded the estate they'd know nothing about it. The boyar is enjoying himself far away—God knows where—perhaps even abroad. While here, a thief like Faliboga guards his riches. Why, Nita, there are funny things in the world. Oh, well. . . . Goodnight. Go and rest."

Lepadatu stopped his horse.

"Uncle Sandu," he said, "wait a bit."

"What's the matter?"

"Uncle Sandu, forgive me for what happened."

"Listen, Nita," said Faliboga laughing. "You are really a man of God. Go to bed; and think about the girl up at the barns instead. . . ."

The bailiff disappeared into the darkness. Lepadatu dismounted and led the horse to shelter. Then he prepared a bed by the side of the beasts. He put away his cudgel at his head and rolled himself up in his sheepskin; he lay thinking, slightly suspicious, over Faliboga's words and behavior, for a long time before going to sleep. A little later his thoughts turned to uncle Nastase's daughter. She appeared to him then as very far off, trembling on uncertain waters, engulfed in the autumn mists and the winds of the coming winter.

Before falling asleep, he heard the mournful cries of strange birds tearing the darkness. . . .

AT THE END of a week the rain had slowed down but the weather was still damp. Heavy whitish mists draped the horizon. The sun was never seen, as if it had passed to other skies, to brighten other worlds. Round the manor house the people of the huts came and went on horseback, leading the cattle to the drinking troughs and bringing them back to their shelters.

Around the sheds and barns the servants went about with difficulty, their clothes rimed with the dampness of the air. Only Faliboga's clamour penetrated, indefatigably, to the farthest corners, while his white mare trotted along the muddy lanes and footpaths.

Nita Lepadatu spent a whole day in the clothing shed, in order to choose pigskin sandals for himself and the boys under his orders, and to see to the mending of sheepskin jackets, with Isaila the furrier. One on top of the other, sandals and sheepskins were heaped up to the very beams of the roof giving off a heavy rancid smell of suet. The two men stood on the dry floor and looked through the wide open door at the cloudy gray distance.

Isaila, an old, bald, dark-faced gipsy with a white

moustache and beard, was sitting with his legs tucked under him, and talking slowly while his needle ran along the edge of a sheepskin.

"My lad," he said, "I used to be a serf in the time of Mr. Iordache, the father of our young boyar. In those days we were settled farther down, on the banks of the Moldova, and working on other estates. There were special bailiffs for the serfs then, who beat us with whips and made us work till we could move neither foot nor hand."

"I've heard tell," said Nita, "that in that region the villages are numerous and near one another."

"Yes, down there, everything's different. Each house has its yard and its garden. Here, in the old days, it was a Tartar country. That's what Anton the miller says."

"Was he rich, our boyar's father?" asked Nita.

The gipsy looked up from his work and nodded.

"Terribly! Lands, cattle, lots of servants . . . then you should have seen the houses . . . big and fine, at Avrameni. . . . The old master had five sons and four daughters. He gave each of them an estate as dowry. Ah, the way Mr. Iordache managed the estates. He was big, with a thick moustache. Everyone was afraid of him. Madame Profira herself trembled when the old master got angry. And now, see what's happened. You'd say the young boyar learned from the old. Mr. Iordache had a certain Neculai the Albanian, as his bailiff at Avrameni; he was a hard worker and bad-tempered, something like our Faliboga. This Neculai, the Albanian, had been a highwayman in his youth, too. He had been sentenced to hard labor and

63

imprisoned too. The boyar got him out and took him on to his estate, so as to frighten people. Because, you know, even in those days the servants were on the lazy side."

The gipsy was looking out through the open door, as if he wanted to call his memories back out of the mists; with a very sharp knife Lepadatu was cutting straps for sandals.

"The boyar's last-born," Isaila resumed, "this little Mr. George, I carried him in my arms, told him stories, taught him to ride a horse. . . . But I was younger then. Now he is grown up, and I am nothing but a poor old man. But he has not forgotten me, and looks after me now. It is only a pity that he is wasting his youth in such a desert. He is a young man and youth has its rights. Here we live in seclusion. For my part I know that tomorrow, or the day after tomorrow, I shall go and join the gipsies and furriers of a hundred years back . . . but he is a boyar in his prime . . . he needs something else, another sort of life fits him."

Outside, near the door, light footsteps and women's voices could be heard.

"Who is it?" asked Isaila between his teeth, as if against his will.

The two men had looked up with the same movement.

After brushing the dirt off their clothes, the nun and Marghiolita, Tentea's daughter, came into the shed. Behind them, with a heavy tread, Anton the German appeared, pipe in mouth, wearing a dirty old cap. His huge beard resembled a handful of red wool mingled with white threads.

64

"Whew," murmured Isaila, "people . . . quite a party we're having. . . ."

The nun gave a quick nod. "Good day! How goes it?"

"I kiss your hand," Isaila mumbled through his beard.

"As you see," added Nita, "we are getting ready for the winter."

He smiled and looked towards Marghiolita. Anton pushed his pipe from one corner to the other of his mouth, and sat down on a heap of sheepskins. He could be heard growling something in his beard.

"*Gootborga, Gootborga,*" answered Isaila laughing and nodding at him.

The German smiled too and took the pipe out of his mouth. He spoke Rumanian with difficulty.

"Vot are you doing, Isaila?"

"What do you think I'm doing, Mr. Anton? I'm sewing skins."

"That's goot, ferry goot!" said the German approvingly, replacing his pipe between his lips.

The nun intervened in her sharp voice. "Uncle Isaila, there must be several fox furs here, which Mr. Anton brought."

"There must, there must," agreed the German.

"They are," answered Isaila. "I looked after them according to the rules. . . . Just what's needed to make you a fine coat."

"Me shot the foxes," mumbled the German from his heap of sheepskins.

"Which means, you killed them and I looked after the furs," Isaila put in.

"Goot, goot!" Anton said, balancing his pipe.

Uncle Isaila put aside the coat that he was sewing, and got up, groaning. He went and rummaged in a dark corner of the shed, and brought out the fox furs. He carried them into the light and unfolded them before the nun. They gleamed tawny and silvery in the dusky evening light.

"Those were fine beasts," Isaila said in a low voice.

"You will bring them to the manor house," the nun told him, shaking her head. She sat down on an upturned bucket. Marghiolita stood beside the nun, her grey shawl on her shoulders, a black kerchief hiding her hair.

The German seemed to be thinking. All at once, as if his pipe was speaking, he groaned: "Me said master would do vell if he was to marry."

"What, to marry?" asked Isaila in surprise.

"There!" the nun burst out, "that's what Mr. Anton thinks. He was in town with our boyar before the rains buying tools . . ."

"Been to Botosani," finished Anton.

"Yes, as far as Botosani. . . . They went to visit other boyars, and Mr. Anton looked and listened . . . and understood that our master was going to get married. . . ."

On the nun's pale face, in her dark eyes, a shadow of distress and anxiety seemed to tremble.

"And to whom, if you please?" asked Isaila, pulling at his furs.

"It's a pig, rich poyar," whined Anton. "He called Master Ionascu. . . . Pig estate at Valeni . . . five thousand acres of forest . . . one single Miss . . ."

"Then it must be Master Ionascu Razu. . . . He used to come to Avrameni in my time, to visit our boyars. I know him, that I do. I've known the daughter too, since she was quite small, a pretty fair-haired little thing. She's Mr. Ionascu's granddaughter."

"So it's true!" murmured the nun, lowering her eyes. "And you even know who it's all about. . . ."

"Of course I know who it's about," Isaila went on gaily. "If I say I knew them. Only Mr. Ionascu must be very old . . . as for Madame I think she is dead."

"*Ja, Ja,*" grunted the German. "Old Madame is no more . . . but young Miss, pretty and sweet like a flower."

"That means . . . hm! that means that now we shall have a mistress!" commented the nun with a strange smile, and looking sidelong at Nita Lepadatu.

The latter winced as if this look had burned him. He was thinking of something else.

Marghiolita put in gently:

"I'm so glad we shall have a young mistress."

"And why, pray?" asked the nun, staring at her.

"I don't know . . . but I've an idea that things will change here!"

"There's no doubt that things will change!" affirmed Isaila. "A young mistress like that—she likes a fine house and stables with high-bred horses. . . . You'll see, our boyar will plant trees and flowers to please her."

"*Ach, ja,*" said the German calmly. "Me paint the carriage."

"That's it!" said Isaila cheerfully to the nun.

"But if she's a well-brought-up young lady how will

she be able to live in such a desert?" asked the nun with a certain irritation. "Anyway, who can live here? There are no parties, nor music, nor theaters as there are in a big town. I know, I do. I've lived in other places. I've even lived at Iasi."

Everyone listened to her in astonishment.

"That's how it must be," murmured Marghiolita, suddenly dreamy.

The nun grinned:

"That's how it is . . . I don't know how I was able to come and bury myself here."

Her malicious smile changed to a joyful laugh, and she looked at Lepadatu again.

"You, Nita, what do you think about it?"

"Eh? What do you expect me to think? If they really love each other then she'll be happy anywhere, even here."

The nun gazed at him for a long time, as though she did not want to take her eyes off his face.

Marghiolita turned away quickly and, her face hidden in shadow, began poking about the shed which was stacked with all sorts of things. She had covered her mouth with her kerchief and was stifling her sighs. The nun leapt to her feet like a spring.

"Well then, uncle Isaila, you'll take the furs and bring them to me at the manor house . . . but first wrap them up in something."

"I'll go now," answered Isaila promptly, dropping his work.

"And you, Nita, come round to me this evening or tomorrow morning. I want to ask you to do me a service."

"Very well," Nita said, looking at her puzzled.

Mr. Anton stood up. "I go make the mill work," he muttered. "I came here, smoked pipe, talked a little, now I go."

"Aren't you coming?" the nun asked Marghiolita.

The girl took a quick step back and murmured: "No, I'm going in . . . father will be waiting for me."

"All right, but try and come to the manor tomorrow."

The nun turned her pale face and dark eyes to the light and went out with a supple, rapid grace. Uncle Isaila loaded the fox furs on to his back, and followed her, walking heavily and more bent than usual.

"Hm," he grumbled to himself, "I must go and find Faliboga and tell him this story of the foxes . . . because if I don't tell him, and if he gets to hear of it, he'll be very angry with me!"

The German seemed to be brooding. He was muttering words that nobody could catch, biting the stem of his pipe. At last he decided to go off, dragging his heavy boots. But on the doorstep he turned back and said in a plaintive, tired tone:

"Vot are you doing, Nita Lepadat? You come to me at the mill. We talk together. My wife dead . . . me alone. Very bored. Ach, we meet again."

He went off puffing at his pipe.

Instantly the shed resumed its usual calm, while the wan light which suffused it seemed to intensify.

Nita at once leaped from his place and approached Marghiolita.

Smiling at her tenderly, he tried to take her hand. She lifted the kerchief which was hiding her eyes and un-

69

covered her face. She drew back and looked at him scared.

"Don't go to the manor house," she begged, speaking fast.

His arms hanging by his side, Nita stood facing her with an inquiring gaze.

"Why, what's the matter?"

Tears shone in Marghiolita's eyes.

"Don't go, Nita—I've only just realized what the nun has in her heart. Don't go."

"But you, Marghiolita, what's the matter with you? Why are you so worried?"

The girl looked at him, with a mixture of anger and love.

She approached him, her hands held out. Nita did not grasp clearly what it was all about, but a thrill ran through his body when he felt her trembling so near him. He took her in his arms, and while she struggled more and more feebly, he kissed her enraptured.

"You won't go, will you, you won't go?" she whispered somehow haggardly. "Come to the hut this evening . . . I'll try and get father out of the way. We'll talk. . . ."

Suddenly she started. A footstep sounded outside, and they heard the nun's sharp voice.

"Marghiolita! Come here! . . . Are you there, Marghiolita?"

Then, more softly: "Don't wait for me, uncle Isaila; go on, I'll catch up to you."

The girl tore herself out of Lepadatu's embrace and put her kerchief on so as to hide her eyes and her mouth. A look of hatred darkened her face. Slipping towards the door she whispered hurriedly: "You'll come this evening, dear. . . ."

Nita was left alone and, as if dazed, he crouched again among the sheepskins which strewed the floor of the shed, near the heap of sandals. He took up the knife and needle to start working again, but it was all in vain. . . .

The dark hut where Marghiolita would be waiting for him rose before his eyes, dazzling him.

Uncle Isaila found him lost in his dreams, staring into space.

When he spoke to him, Nita started.

"I've been to the manor house. If you could just see our nun's room! Only the most expensive carpets. . . . But what's the matter, my boy? You don't seem quite yourself."

"There's nothing wrong, uncle Isaila," answered Nita laughing. "I was only thinking of something."

The old man smiled knowingly.

"I know what you are thinking about, my boy. When I was your age I thought about the same things."

"Well, uncle, I wasn't thinking about what you imagine!"

"Yes, yes," insisted Isaila, the furrier. "I can see by the look on your face. Anyway, it's not my business. I was thinking of something myself . . . of my own worries."

The old man bent once more over the fur, and began humming a tune through his nose. After a few minutes he raised his voice, in a drawling, melancholy tone:

"Don't pay any attention, my lad, to these words. It's a song of yore."

They caught each other's eye, and both burst out

71

laughing. Then both looked out towards the sad fields, drowned in mist.

As far as Nita Lepadatu knew, Marghiolita was not a girl like the others. She was violent in her love and it seemed that her intelligence was sharpened thereby. Sometimes, at night, when he went to her, and the old man was not there, he was left giddy after their embraces, while Marghiolita calmly lit a miserable lamp, put it on the edge of the hearth and began chattering and asking him all sorts of questions as to what might happen in their lives.

"This is what I think," she said once. "We'll go and see our boyar, in the spring, and we'll let him know that we want to get married. . . . We'll ask him to help us to settle down, to start a decent home like there are in other parts, as we've heard tell."

Lepadatu marvelled at such thoughts; but they did not in any way displease him.

"And there will have to be a proper wedding—at church, and with a priest. The people here have forgotten those things."

"You're right," agreed Nita. "We must be married like true Christians, before God . . . and we'll have to go to the Registrar's Office too."

"We'll go if we must," said Marghiolita pensively.

Another time, when they were parting, Nita remembered something and began to laugh.

"Tell me, Marghiolita," he said, "what was the matter with you that day in the shed, when you kept begging me not to go to the nun at the manor?"

"Did you go?"

"I didn't, but it surprised me. It looked as though you hated her. But you go to her, and Madame wishes you well."

"Oh, never mind. It was nothing. It was just a whim."

"I didn't go, and maybe she was annoyed. I thought there was something . . ."

Marghiolita laughed lightly and buried her face in the young man's breast.

"If she was annoyed it must have passed off. Oh, forget about the nun!"

Returning to his beasts, Nita thought: "The girl is a sly she-devil. Why does she tease me now and keep me dangling? I can't do anything about it. She sees that I love her, and so. . . ."

Some time later, a cold wind from the north swept the clouds and mist away and a yellowish sun shone feebly.

The puddles of water and mud coagulated. And one evening the sky, still bronzed by the sunset, was overcast with clouds, clouds which were heavy with snow. A storm blowing from the frozen lakes began to send the first flakes whirling down.

Winter was setting in with a snowstorm.

At night, Faliboga came round to Nita's stable.

"The winter is not starting as usual," said he. "A bad sign, my friend."

"Yes," replied the lad, "winters are hard times. There is nothing we can do about it. It's God's will."

"Have you got a good sheepskin jacket? Are your pig-skin sandals thick and strong enough? You'll be able to turn your back on the winter till it's over."

"What else could be done?" said Nita, with a laugh.

The bailiff went off to the other stables.

Now life swarmed more thickly round the manor house. The shepherds brought up their flocks of sheep and distributed them in different pens. The cattle were herded into the stables.

For fear of winter all the boyar's riches were concentrated in a single spot. It seemed that the first breath of ill wind had shaken everybody. People came and went on this first winter evening, talked loud, called each other, shouted, and swore at their dogs.

Nita Lepadatu turned his coat inside out, with the fur outside; he walked slowly past the long rows of beasts, made sure that they needed nothing and that they were quiet, then whistled for Sarmanu, the dog, which had been given him by the boys under his orders.

He drew a huge chunk of cold maize porridge out of his cloak and put it down for the dog.

"Hey Sarmanu! have you got a coat for the winter?" said he, patting its neck and muzzle.

The dog's thick black coat shone against the whirling snowflakes. Nita stood for quite a time, wrapped in his thoughts, looking out into the darkness.

Ever since he had lived near animals belonging to all sorts of boyars, and as far back as his memory would allow, he could remember that the first shivers of winter filled his soul with a strange disquiet, something like an oppressive bitterness, like a grinding of hatred which came over him from an unknown world.

"Let's go to the huts, Sarmanu!" he said to the dog.

With the coat on his shoulders and the dog a few steps behind him, Nita went forward through the fluttering snowflakes.

One could just make out the dim lights winking from the people's burrows.

He went in to the old men's hut and took a seat on the bench by the fire. The dog lay down at his feet. The young man sat thinking for a while. From time to time a tired servant or a shepherd covered with snow, came in, smoked a pipe and went off again. The old men talked among themselves with an anxious note in their voices, and evoked the hardest winters they had known in their lives. It was as if they were talking of wars or other similar misfortunes. Every time they paused, the roaring of the storm could be heard outside. The gusts of wind which came down the chimney shook the flickering flame of the lamp.

The storm calmed down the next morning, but it went on snowing for another day and night. As soon as the last flake had fallen the cold became sharper. The people of the huts emerged from their dwellings as if from the depths of the earth, and started tracing paths and tracks in the deep bed of snow.

The smoke rose vertically from the roofs of the huts, and the noises and voices echoed and re-echoed as if under a vault of thick glass.

Faliboga and Lepadatu went off to inspect the huge ricks of straw and hay which had been prepared for the winter. From these, the servants ceaselessly loaded their sledges. Round the pens where the sheep had been installed, the shepherds were clearing away heaps of snow. Everything, to the farthest horizon, was white, immaculately, spotlessly white. A shadow descended from time to time and dissolved near the ground: it was a procession of rooks, marking the luminous sheet of snow with black moving dots.

Two DAYS before St. Nicholas' day, towards noon, a silvery sound of sleigh-bells could be heard from the top of the hills, in the direction of the barns. Like a powder-train the rumor spread that Mr. George Avrameanu, the boyar, was coming back. Ant-like, the people of the huts appeared from all directions. Even women and bare-footed children came out of their shelters, pushing and craning their necks to see.

It was indeed the master, coming back in a sledge drawn by four horses with bells merrily jingling. Faliboga and Jana appeared on the threshold of their hut wearing clean coats over their shoulders, and went down to the manor house to meet the boyar.

"Oh, Sandu!" cried the bailiff's woman admiringly. "I've never seen such a fine sledge!"

"Be quiet!" retorted Faliboga laughing. "There's something even better and finer inside the sledge."

"What is it?"

"It's true . . . I'm taller than you, and my neck's longer. Stretch up on tiptoe and see for yourself."

"Oh, Sandu! It's she that will be our mistress . . . what a beautiful lady."

Mr. George had returned to his land, with his bride and with the old boyar Ionascu Razu.

"So, Jana," murmured Faliboga, "after all, it was true that we said. Who knows what will happen now?"

Jana turned to her man and looked at him sideways, frowning slightly.

"Why do you say that, Sandu?"

"Ah, Jana, that dove is a town bird. You'll see, she'll end up by taking our master away from this desert of ours."

Jana gave no answer. She fixed her burning eyes on the sledge now advancing slowly and she carefully studied the young lady's rosy face, framed in furs.

Then she sheltered behind Faliboga's back and pulled her big sheepskin coat tighter around her.

"We shall soon see what the deuce comes of it," she whispered gently.

The sledge drew up before the steps of the log house. The white curtains moved at the windows as though eyelids were being lowered, raised, and lowered again. . . . At last the door opened, and, tiny in her fox fur coat, the nun appeared on the threshold; she looked with a fixed smile at the delicate face of the newcomer. From all sides, the people of the huts were arriving in groups, gathering round the sledge, cap in hand.

Mr. George was the first to disengage himself from the mass of furs and coats; he jumped swiftly down to the ground, a happy smile on his beaming face.

The old boyar followed him, heavy and fat, with a white moustache and black eyebrows. Finally, with the help of Mr. George's arms, the fair-haired little lady got down—she was lighter than a butterfly, a white toque was pulled over one eye, and her cheeks were buried in a fur-like down.

They entered the house. Bowing respectfully, the nun brought up the rear. Outside, the servants and the people of the huts stood respectfully. They contemplated the sledge, the horses and the coachman who was swaggering about in his blue fur-lined coat, his head adorned by a Cossack fur cap.

Then, when the carriage had turned off towards the stables, they waited about yet awhile, talking among themselves of boyars and of the marvellous countries whence these happy and well-nourished beings came. All this was like a burst of sunshine, like the arrival of a king, in their dreary lives.

When the boyars came out again, the mud-hut dwellers stood in two lines, watching them with admiring attention. The former were ruddy cheeked and in high spirits. Mr. George came up to his subjects and said with a smile:

"Good people, here is your mistress."

He too looked at the two beautiful eyes which kept twinkling in her face, as at something very precious.

"May God give her good health! May God bless her!" several voices replied.

The old boyar was smoking, using an amber cigarette-holder. He looked at the people gathered round, absent-mindedly. Then, addressing the fair-haired lady, he murmured with a pitiful smile:

"Oh! ils sont bien sales, les pauvres gens."

79

"What is he saying?" whispered the hut dwellers, turning to each other.

Wrapping themselves in their gleaming furs, the boyars came forward several paces. At the sight of the huts they stopped. The fair lady burst out laughing:

"Tiens! qu'est-ce que c'est que ça?"

And with a tender look at Mr. George, she went on, still in French:

"Ah, they are houses! How very queer they look!"

"Indeed, we are a long way from civilization here!" added Mr. Ionascu, puffing a bluish cloud of smoke around him.

"It's very strange . . . really very strange!" murmured the lady, her eyes suddenly cloudy. "These huts remind me of the stories about charcoal burners that I used to read at the French school which I attended."

The people of the huts followed the boyars at a good distance, timidly, like a satisfied herd. The masters turned towards the cattle-pens and stables.

"My farming is very sketchy," Mr. George whispered with an embarrassed smile. "But we can't help it. You must not forget that we are on new land here."

The young lady kept her eyes on him, smiling sweetly all the time.

She was really very beautiful and exquisite and the people of the huts stared at her, taking in every detail with astonishment and wonder and telling each other their impressions, in low voices.

"They are talking French," murmured Faliboga to Jana.

"I don't think it can be very nice here, even in summer," cooed the lady pivoting gracefully on her heels.

"Personally, I think," said Avrameanu, "that nothing could be nicer than cornfields. . . . Hullo, there's Faliboga."

He had just caught sight of the bailiff.

"Come here, Sandu," he called out at once.

Faliboga approached, rather stiff, and trying as best he could to soften the surly expression of his face.

"We kiss your hand, mistress!" he said humbly holding out his heavy black paw.

"Give him your hand to kiss," murmured Mr. George, still in French.

Faliboga raised his eyes and looked first at the master, then kissed the little gloved hand held out to him.

"Well, Sandu," the boyar asked kindly, "is everything going all right here?"

"Everything's all right, master!" Faliboga answered quietly. "Just like every other year. I'll come to the manor and report."

"We have no time now, Sandu," said Avrameanu, "we are only passing through. We are leaving tomorrow morning."

"Are you going far, master?"

"Yes, a good way. . . . We are going to Italy. You've not even heard of it."

"Why, yes, master, it does happen that we have heard of it," said Faliboga with a sigh, glancing at Jana.

The young lady suddenly began to laugh.

81

"I'm cold! I'm cold!" she sighed. "Let's go in, may we?" She took Avrameanu's arm and put her head on his shoulder. "There, I've agreed to your wish . . . and we have come to visit your kingdom at the end of the earth . . ." and laughed lightly. "But, for heaven's sake, let's go now, quick! quick! and far away . . . where there are flowers . . . and songs. . . . Ah, George, how happy I am. . . ."

They quickened their steps. The old boyar strove painfully to catch up with them, and looked rather annoyed. In a low voice he grumbled and scolded:

"Be sensible, Rozina, the people are looking at you." Finally he began to cough and threw away his cigarette.

With an admiring smile on her lips, Jana followed the new mistress with her eyes; she remarked to her man:

"Did you hear that, Sandu? Her name's Zina."

Faliboga grunted something unintelligible. The boyars went into the house.

A little later, Mr. George came out alone, called his bailiff and said in a loud voice:

"Listen, Sandu! Send a man with a sledge to the village. He must go to the pub and bring back twelve gallons of brandy. You will distribute them to the people on my behalf. This very evening. But you must take care."

"I understand, master. And . . . when are you coming back?"

"Who?" asked the boyar surprised. "Ah, yes, the lady doesn't like it here very much . . . but I'll come back soon . . . as soon as I possibly can."

"Then I wish you a good journey, master, and a safe return."

A minute white hand was knocking on the inside of the window. Mr. George looked around laughing and went in.

Frowning, Faliboga rejoined the servants, who were waiting outside. "You can cover your heads!" he grunted between his teeth. He himself replaced his fur cap on his head and pulled it down over his ears.

"Let Andrei Broasca go and fetch brandy," he cried with his usual roughness. "You others, back to your work. The boyars are at home now, and resting. What more do you want now?"

Little by little the people of the huts scattered as they went dragging their straw-stuffed sandals through the snow, and commenting on the great event. Faliboga hailed one of the boys.

"Hey, Grecusor! Off with you and saddle my mare. I want to go and see if they carried out the orders I gave this morning."

He went off grumbling in one direction, while Grecusor scampered away in the other, with great bounds over the heaps of snow.

With his dog at his heels, Nita Lepadatu had waited for the masters' arrival near the cow-house. He had seen them coming towards him, and had taken his hat off when they were still far away. But the shining eyes in the foam of white fur had barely glanced at him, immediately flying off and resting elsewhere. The boyars had gone off again and Nita, cap in hand, had stayed there rooted to the spot.

Quickening his step, Faliboga came up to him and

chuckled: "Well, Nita! What do you think of it all? . . . For God's sake, man, put on your cap."

"How tiny and beautiful she is!" said Nita.

"But what did you think she'd be? She's a pure being—not like us, who smell of earth and dung and the smoke of the huts. She's a creature—how can I tell you?—made of cream! . . . a creature that has grown up wrapped in down . . . well, of a different race."

Lepadatu was silent. He looked straight in front of him, and smiled as though his eyes were riveted to some sweet vision.

The next morning, in the silence of the valley, the sleigh-bells could be heard tinkling with different sounds. The frost had abated, and the sun was shining in a clear blue sky. The four straining horses halted, with the sledge full of furs and covers, at the foot of the house steps, while on the driver's seat the coachman sat, upright and superb, not deigning to give the slightest look around him. The people of the huts gathered around again, waiting for the masters' departure. In the veranda behind the house, Faliboga was talking to Mr. George, answering all his questions and receiving orders.

When the bailiff came out, everyone looked towards the barns up on the hills. A narrow sledge was hurrying down from there, drawn by a little horse. Faliboga shaded his eyes with his hand to see better.

"It must be the mayor," he growled, without budging from his place.

The little black horse trotted along swiftly. It came up to the manor and stopped. A shortish, paunchy man edged out of the sleigh. He was wearing a sheepskin coat; between its broad collar and the high pointed fur cap, a thick, ruddy face emerged. Two small eyes looked inquiringly about.

"Who will look after the horse and the covers for me?" he asked in a fat man's thick voice. He took off his thick woollen mittens, threw back his cap and pulled the collar of his coat down flat on his shoulders.

"What wind brings you here, sir?" inquired Faliboga.

The government official turned around, his thick lips slightly parted in a smile.

"Ah, it's you, Mr. Sandu? The boyars are here, aren't they? I saw them yesterday as they passed through the village."

"Yes, they are here," said Faliboga accompanying his words with a nod of his head. "Now we have a mistress too."

"I know, I know," the mayor said with a laugh. "That's why I hurried to come and pay my respects."

The people of the huts followed the scene in silence.

The mayor stood looking about for a few minutes, then fixed his gaze on the manor house.

"This way," said Faliboga with a wave of his hand. "By the back. . . ."

But the front-door opened wide, and the boyars appeared, wrapped in their furs. The mayor rushed forward towards the steps. Mr. George at once recognized him, and said, slightly surprised: "Why, it's Mr. Valcu! How long have you been here?"

"I arrived this very moment!" answered the mayor, bowing very low to the boyar's lady.

"A moment, mayor, a moment. . . ."

Mr. George helped his young wife to climb into the sledge and buried her under a mountain of covers. She watched him with her shining eyes, while a tender smile floated on her fresh red lips.

"What glorious weather!" she twittered. "Come on, George! Come, do let us get on."

"A moment," whispered Avrameanu in French. "I must have a word or two with this man."

The old boyar heaved himself into the sledge, in his turn. The nun stood with downcast eyes, motionless and respectful in the veranda.

The master went up to the mayor and drew him aside. They talked for a few minutes, in low voices. Finally, Avrameanu opened his fur coat, plunged a hand into his pocket and brought out a wallet. He selected a long blue banknote which Mr. Valcu lost no time in pocketing.

"Thank you very much," said the mayor with a broad smile. "As always, I am at your service. . . ."

"Good, good!" Avrameanu replied quickly, looking away and re-buttoning his fur coat. "Good-bye, Mr. Valcu! Good-bye."

"Your servant," said the mayor, bowing rather lower to the white fur.

The lady winked only, and Mr. George made haste to get into the sledge. The nun ran down from the veranda.

Faliboga approached too on the other side. The coachman turned around and they all did their best to arrange the furs and covers.

"Sandu," said Mr. George once more, "see that everything goes properly."

Faliboga took off his cap.

"Don't be afraid, master. . . . Farewell!"

All the mud-hut dwellers removed their caps.

"Good-bye!" called out Mr. George for the last time. "Off we go, Costache!"

The coachman cracked his whip, the bells on the horses' necks began to tinkle again, and the sledge leaped lightly forward towards the hills. Behind, gradually more and more outdistanced, Mr. Valcu hastened home, wrapped up in his covers, his hat pulled down over his eyes and his coat collar pulled up. Only the tip of his nose was visible.

"Well, Nita!" said Faliboga to Lepadatu, "now you have seen the government official in person . . . the mayor of the nearest village. He's an old fox, is Mr. Valcu. Whenever he smells the boyar is back, he loses no time. . . . Apart from that whoever sees him? Our master slipped a little blue note into his paws, and there you are. He calls that doing his duty. Apart from this occasional visit we live on our own—without any mayor, without any priest. The tax-collector also comes once a year, and it's always to look for money. After that it's all over."

Faliboga laughed, as his eyes followed the little wooden sledge which was trying hard to keep pace with the big handsome sledge of the boyars.

"But you, Nita," he added immediately, "how you were gaping . . . like yesterday. You seemed to have seen a fairy, like the ones they talk about in tales. Come along, put on your cap."

The soft sound of the sleigh-bells soon faded in the

distance, while the manor and the huts, more lonely and more dismal now than previously, were again wrapped up in the wintry silence.

The bailiff went off to see to his business, while Nita, his dog beside him, returned to his cattle. But towards evening, all the mud-hut dwellers gathered round the fire, began again to talk about the extraordinary event and about this vision from another world, which had appeared for a moment in their sunless existence. . . .

THE WINTER continued, peaceful and slow. Men and beasts lived, on the whole, not too badly. Nothing else disturbed the solitude of the lonely settlement. Only once, the day before Christmas Eve, a priest and a sexton from the church of Mr. Valcu's village came on horseback to announce the birth of the Saviour to the people of the huts. They went first to the manor house, where they were received by the nun, looking more devout and sadder than ever. Then they passed on to the huts, giving their blessing to the women and children whom they happened to meet on the way.

Faliboga did his duty to them, and towards midday the priest and the sexton went home again, trotting along on their little horses across the white stretch of snow. The people followed them with their eyes till they had disappeared like two black dots in the distance.

At Christmas everyone ate pork and drank brandy as was the custom. They knew that a new year was about to begin, and celebrated it in the warmth of the huts. The shepherds too had their share of eating and drinking, as did the men who kept watch in the beasts' pens. Till dawn

Faliboga rushed about in all directions, without a moment's rest, seeing that nobody was smoking in the straw or among the thatch, that nobody had fallen down among the beasts. Everybody was allowed to have a drop too much on such occasions; but drunkenness can sometimes also have its dangers.

One evening after Epiphany, while Faliboga and Lepadatu were chatting in the old men's hut, the north wind rose again.

"Up to now," said Faliboga, "we have come out of the first half of winter not too badly. We'll see now what the other half is like."

"Bah!" replied Nita, laughing, "this winter can't be any different from the others. It will be as it will be."

"That's true. The winter has never yet been eaten up by wolves. Yet, you see, no sooner has Epiphany gone by than I begin thinking about the spring. In winter, staying so much at home, you get suffocated. Jana's the same . . . she longs for the spring sun."

Faliboga nestled near the fire. Mihalache Prescurie put in:

"In springtime the master will come back—with the storks."

Faliboga shook his head and sighed.

"How good it is when the snow begins to melt, and the green fields show themselves . . . when the lark goes up to the very top of the sky, singing. Streams come to life everywhere and are white with foam. And it smells, I don't know how . . . a sweet smell. Even my mare trembles with impatience and happiness and neighs when I ride her. Mr. George takes his horse too, and we go off, the two of us, to decide which corner is to be worked, which fields are to be left for pasture . . . where the hay is to be made. . . . Oh, he loves the black earth, does our boyar—just like me."

"But, Sandu," said uncle Irimia Izdrail, from his corner. "I'll tell you something, I will. How could he help loving this earth of ours? I've seen a good few places in my life and a lot of earth has trickled through my fingers. But here there's something else. Here the earth is so fine . . . God made it like that—that the harvests it gives are like nothing anyone has seen or heard of in this world. Here the maize grows higher than a man on horseback. The wheat comes up to your shoulders. And you wouldn't find bigger or heavier ears of corn. . . . How should I know? God blessed this earth, that's certain."

"That's why our boyar never wanted to live anywhere else," murmured Faliboga. "That's why he always lived here in our desert, as if he was in love with it. From morning till night, he used to roam the fields with me. Towards the middle of summer we'd go together to the market-town of Saveni, when the harvesters from the farthest villages collected there and the prices for labor were fixed. We brought back people as if it had been for a fair . . . and they went off straight away with their sickles across the fields. You would have said it was an army. And, Nita, that's why our boyar always liked it here, you see, among the wealth that the harvesters cut and tied in sheaves. It's true . . . the earth here is blessed."

Gheorghe Barba, at the other end of the hut, spoke in his turn.

"I agree with you; at harvest time it's good to live here.

91

Men and women . . . all the barns full . . . and then there's laughing, there's singing . . . the evening near the fires. It's always like that when there are plenty of people about."

"Confess, Barba, confess," cut in Faliboga, teasing him. "Confess that's what you like best. You sing and joke with the girls. You remember the time when you were young."

"What's the use of joking!" grumbled Gheorghe Barba. "I'm nothing but an old man. There's nothing like youth, as the song says. . . ."

Everyone began to laugh. Uncle Irimia nodded to Lepadatu.

"A lad like him can have a good time in summer."

"Who knows?" answered Nita, "I may be thinking of something else next summer."

"But why, my lad?"

"That," said Faliboga, "is a secret . . . and you're not supposed to know it, uncle. . . . Till then I should not be surprised if Gheorghe Barba might play his flute for somebody's wedding."

They were all silent. Nobody asked any more questions. Only uncle Irimia mumbled with a sigh: "With God's help. . . ."

The wind could be heard blowing down the chimney. "We're going to have bad weather," observed Mihalache Prescurie.

Silence fell again. After a moment Sandu resumed in his gruff voice:

"Hm, I wonder where they are now, our boyars? Who knows where they are. They say that the Italians' country

92

is somewhere where the sea itself is warm; it never rains there. It's always springtime. That's what the boyar once said to me. We were on horseback in the fields and he was talking to me and telling me all sorts of things."

"Who knows where that country is!" said Nita.

"If it is on the edge of the sea," said Mihalache Prescurie, "then it must be on the edge of the earth, where the swallows and the storks spend the winter. But what surprises me is how men can get there."

"Why, easily enough," said Faliboga, laughing. "Nowadays there are trains . . . you go quick as lightning."

After another moment's silence, Nita asked: "Do the people over there live better than here?"

Faliboga answered with a grin:

"Rather! Otherwise, why do you think our boyars have gone there—except to live better? If I could I should fly from the winter in the same way. Although I don't know why I should—now that I've got used to it."

"I think," said Nita, "that the boyar has gone only to please his lady. . . . so dainty and white. I must say that I'd never seen such a beautiful creature before. It must have been she who dragged the boyar away. Didn't you notice how he looked at her? Like at a jewel! Maybe at this very moment they are talking and enjoying themselves."

They heard the wind again, raging and roaring down the chimney. The flame of the oil-lamp quivered and nearly went out.

The bailiff stood up and started looking for his whip and his fur cap.

"I'll go and see what's going on outside," he said.

"I'll go too," whispered Nita, rising in his turn and putting his sheepskin coat on his shoulders. "The boys must be waiting for me."

As soon as they were outside the hut, the wind blew the icy flakes in their faces. But a little further on, the storm seized them in a whirl of snow.

"Damn it all!" shouted Faliboga, spitting and wiping his mouth. "It gets right inside your throat."

Nita wrapped himself up in his big sheepskin.

Faliboga went down to the hut. "It's no good," he groaned, "I'll have to go and get something thicker on. . . . You, Nita, don't go away from the beasts tonight. With such a storm, who knows what might happen."

"Even on other nights I always sleep beside them," replied Nita as he left the bailiff.

At first he had an idea of going up to the barns, to uncle Nastase's hut, to see Marghiolita and have a talk with her.

But, the next moment, he made for his stable. Something unusual was happening on earth and in the air. The wind was loaded with thousands upon thousands of needles.

The fine snow penetrated into the slightest folds of the clothes. In the sky, something like an immense torrent seemed to be roaring and rushing.

When he got near the stable, Nita realized that the wind had grown stronger. He found the boys huddled in a corner, waiting for him. His dog leaped up when he caught sight of his master and began to rub against his legs. The beasts were standing motionless in the dark.

Nita felt that they were restless, their heads up and their ears cocked.

The snow tapped with a dry sound on the willow palings of the pens. Flakes penetrated through the gaps and the roof. From time to time a gust of wind beat heavily against the fragile partitions, hissing furiously, and flapping its vast invisible wings.

"Uncle Nita," said Nistor, one of the boys, "the wolves are sure to come again tonight to the cattle-pens."

"Be quiet, you! and don't talk nonsense. Our dogs will make short work of them if they do . . . and we've got guns too. Anyway, in weather like this even wolves daren't leave their lairs."

"Uncle, how will you stay here alone? Listen to what's happening outside . . . it sounds like the end of the world."

"Why, lads!" said Nita gently, "I see the storm has scared you as it used to scare me when I was your age. Never mind, get to bed."

Huddling together, the boys went off to their hut, carefully closing the rush door behind them. Nita went past the rows of beasts right up to the end of the stable, listening attentively to their breathing. Then he came back towards the corner where he usually made his bed. He kept a gun there, which was always loaded. But as he had more faith in his brass-headed cudgel he took this out and placed it so that he could have it close at hand. It was only after these precautions that he rolled himself up in his sheepskin and lay down.

For a long time he lay on his back, thinking. He was not sleepy, and around the pens the storm was raging. He began thinking about his childhood and about the life spent among all sorts of strangers. He could not call to mind either his father or his mother; a little later he thought of his love and again had the feeling that Marghiolita was standing there, smiling and real, at the head of his bed.

Behind him, through the rush wall, the wind blew in a fine dust of snow; while the darkness surrounding him seemed to be filled with the visions and shadowy figures of his dreams. . . .

And suddenly, as he raised himself on an elbow, he thought he perceived a strange, long drawn-out shuddering.

"This wind is unusually strong," he thought.

Now there was no pause, no respite. An unimaginable, superhuman fury seemed to have broken loose and was about to lift the stable and carry it away. An endless whining pierced the air, resounding to the ends of the horizon like a cry of horror from what had previously been silence and calm.

"The storm is shaking the foundations of the world . . ." whispered Nita, shivering.

The beasts began to be restless and huddled together.

Sarmanu growled as if it had heard someone approaching.

"Be quiet, it's nobody!" Nita said.

He got up and tried to see through the darkness what was happening. He wondered what to do to calm the beasts. But they, as well as the dog, had felt something and had felt it earlier than the man.

And when the man felt it, it was too late.

With sudden sharp noises the stable began creaking with all its joints.

Terrified in a jostling turmoil, the beasts ran against one another and hit the rush walls. Pushed by the heavy wave, assailed from outside by the storm, the stable began to give way. Now the roaring beasts plunged through the gaps and escaped. Sarmanu gave an almost human cry of despair.

A mass of thatch like a huge wing suddenly hit Lepadatu. Stunned by the shock and thinking he might have to defend himself against a human enemy, he bent down to find his cudgel. But the wind broke through a nearby gap in the wall, and a whirlwind of snow blinded him.

It had all lasted an instant.

The beasts went on roaring in the surrounding fields. Nita, who had fallen on all fours, had not time to get up.

The roofing of thatch and straw came away completely and dropped heavily down, crushing him beneath its weight. He had the feeling that he was lost.

For a moment he could still hear his dog howling. Then the wind drowned his cries of distress and his appeals for help.

Faliboga, returning home on his mare, through the gusts of wind, heard the roaring of the beasts, the piercing cries and the crashing of the stable. Hurriedly he left the path and began shouting in his hoarse voice:

"Hey, Nita, where are you? What's happened?"

He got off his mare and rushed forward through the drifting snow. The snow blinded him. He felt the ground with his hands and feet. Then he stopped abruptly, and listened hard: there was no doubt about it, someone, near-by, had just given a moan. He hesitated a second. Ought he not first to run to the huts and give the alarm? But he did not pause to reflect. He began again searching the dark-ness, and throwing off the rushes and straw of the ruined stable, to left and right. From time to time he stopped to listen. He shouted again: "Hey, Nita! where are you? It's me, lad! don't you hear me?"

Now the groans sounded nearer and more distinct. Fali-boga began to yell towards the huts: "Hey, down there! Wake up, for God's sake!"

Then a thought crossed his mind. He tore off the rifle which he carried slung over his shoulder and let off two shots. The reports mixed with the seething of the wild wind.

Faliboga bent down again scratching his hands, till, panting desperately, he felt a sheepskin—Nita's coat. Rolled up in it, the young man's body was still warm.

The bailiff drew it out as best he could from the mass of beams and rushwork, and wrapped it up in the sheep-skin. Then he leaped on to his mare, galloped towards the huts and started shouting in his terrible voice.

That night of horror and desolation, Nita very nearly died.

He was carried to the old men's hut: his skull was split and his legs broken. They brought Jana to make him poultices of bread soaked in brandy and to put a little wax candle near his head. The old men watched beside him till morning. He moaned ceaselessly with closed eyes.

The day had scarcely dawned when Marghiolita arrived as though brought by the storm which was still raging. She burst out crying, clasping her head with her hands, then fell down, her face to the ground, beside the bench on which her beloved lay.

For three days and three nights, Nita, whose body was crushed, did not come to his senses. Then, at last, the dim light which filtered into the hut began to shine brighter in his half-closed eyes. . . .

❁   ❁   ❁

It was a peasant from the village of Bordeeni who told me recently all these tales of the times when the Prut region was deserted.

One summer day I had reached the village where this man was mayor, and I had stopped in the yard of his house, which was surrounded by a wicker fence.

He gave my horses shelter in a stable with whitewashed mud walls spotted with blue, and invited me on to the terrace of his house to rest.

He was a robust man with long hair, a short greying moustache and eyes buried under bushy brows. I noticed that he walked somewhat to one side; he had a slight limp.

He very affably offered me a drink of cold water to quench my thirst. Meanwhile, in honor of the visitors, his wife added a well-fattened hen to the beetroot soup which was cooking for the evening meal. Two lively, restless little boys came and went, busied themselves with the work of the house, and running hither and thither from the spotlessly clean shed to the cattle-pen.

99

It was only much later, after I had eaten my meal, that the man came to sit down a few paces away on the terrace and called his wife. He spoke in a quiet voice.

"Marghiolita, come and have a glass of wine too!"

When the woman had returned to her loom, the peasant, Nita Lepadatu, began telling me about the life he had led on the estate of the boyar George Avrameanu. He told me about everything, including the terrible night when he nearly died, and his sufferings, which had lasted till the springtime.

"But in the spring," he went on, looking at me with a smile, "I left the hut and went to sit in the warm sunshine. And when the swallows began to come back and the field flowers started to bloom, my troubles were over. Then the boyar came home too, and Marghiolita and I, we asked him and his lady to come to our wedding.

"D'you know, we had to go all the way to Iasi to get married. The lady did not want to see our desert again, but she consented to come to our wedding . . . in reward for my faithful service and for what I had suffered while they were enjoying themselves and making merry by the shores of the sea which is always warm.

"We travelled over a good stretch of country that time and saw quite a few towns and villages . . . and when we got back, our estate and the piece of land that our master had given us, seemed, oh, so deserted and forsaken! And because we had seen so many things, houses and farms and trains and goodness knows what else—we thought that we ought to do our best and get out of the hut . . .

and we built ourselves a house . . . and many did so after us. . . . But our master, poor man, after a time, never came back here any more. He did what his lady wished and went and bought another estate, and these fields fell into other hands. They were broken up, all sorts of people owned them one after the other, and the old inhabitants acquired some parts too: many of those who were born and lived in these huts managed to settle on their own plot of land, and built a real house for themselves . . . so that today we have, as you might say, a bit of village, and we are no longer so far from the world."

While Nita Lepadatu was telling me all this, other villagers were returning from the fields along the road which passed his door, and several lads were singing, their voices rising steady and gay in the calm of the evening.

I looked all around, across the surrounding country, at the hills where golden corn was gently rippling in the breeze, at the little valleys reserved for pasture, and at the endless stubble-field stretching to the south. I asked my host:

"What became of the old manor house?"

"It was pulled down and another one built, rather higher up. Then the second too remained without a master, and was pulled down too. The other boyars had a fine brick house built over there in the middle of the estate. They changed the manors and their sites just as they used to change the cattle-pens, nearly every year. But now even the cattle-pens are not changed as often, and they build them as they should."

Nita Lepadatu smiled and added: "I've heard it said that they are making the train run not far from here, in the Jijia valley."

"Yes, it's true," I said. "Why, that's the way things change in this world. But Faliboga? What become of Faliboga and his Jana?"

Nita sat musing for a while:

"Well, you see," he answered, "Faliboga was a queer sort of man, as he used to say himself. He was like a wild horse. When he saw that the population went on increasing, that one master followed another, each more cruel and greedy than the last, he and Jana jumped on to their horses and crossed the Prut. They went who knows where? Nobody has ever heard of them again. Vanished like the trail of a bird."

He gazed for a while at the light violet mist that was gathering in the distance.

"If it had not been for Faliboga," he said at last, "I should certainly have died during that awful night. To tell you the truth, for myself I never had much faith in him . . . but he had a good heart. Every year I have a mass said for his soul. Perhaps he is not alive any longer. Perhaps he has already gone where we shall all go some day."

This is how Nita Lepadatu talked to me that summer evening. And when I had heard all there was to know about the people of those days, about the old men and about the nun and all the other people who had lived in the mud huts, satisfied as if I had just read one of those

stories where you are told how each hero lived and died—
the good as well as the bad. . . . And, just as after reading
a good tale, it was a long time before I could get to
sleep . . . and while I lay thinking, the shadows of the past
mingled with the fragrance of the bundle of hay on which
my head was resting. . . .

BIOGRAPHICAL SKETCH
of the Author

On October 19, 1961, Mihail Sadoveanu, former president of the Rumanian Presidium and widely revered as his country's foremost writer, died at the age of eighty-one.

For half a century and more Mihail Sadoveanu's matchless works and his talent as prose writer have had a commanding influence over Rumanian literature. A great story-teller, a consummate master of the Rumanian language, a careful observer of facts, his work is a unique and vital expression of the joy and suffering of his people to whom he was bound in devoted affection.

Sadoveanu was born on November 5, 1880, at Pascani, a humble little town in the north of Moldavia, with a population consisting of a large number of needy people, a downtrodden world. He was brought up under his father's strict supervision and under the wise and protecting care of his mother, a peasant from Verseni, a village on the banks of the river Moldova. It was from her that Sadoveanu inherited his poetic taste for folk tales; it was thanks to her that he grew fond of all those who live in ignorance, misery and oppression.

"Among the few joys experienced by my mother during her short life"—Sadoveanu owned in the speech delivered at the Academy of the Rumanian People's Republic on the occasion of his 70th birthday—"I must mention my rising into a new life, the life of people who can read and write, and I must confess that in my mother's family I was the first to enter this order of the elect. Should my work represent a valuable contribution in the eyes of my fellow citizens, I am bound to pass on all your praise—which I whole-heartedly accept—to the downtrodden people and all those persecuted by fate, to all those who have passed away, as flowers and leaves pass away every season, and who handed down to me a wealth of values created by heart and mind in order that, one day, I should present it to the appreciation of a new world, as a striking evidence of the immense injustice they have suffered, of the unforgivable crime that was perpetrated against them by all oppressors."

The consciousness of this task to accomplish has inspired Mihail Sadoveanu all his life; that is why his work is a hymn of love dedicated to the Rumanian people and a passionate appeal to fight for their onward march into light. Sadoveanu has enriched Rumanian literature with more than one hundred and twenty volumes.

His first book of tales and his first historical novel, *The Falcons*, belong to 1904. A year later the writer published *Tales of War*; then, in 1906, memories of barrack life were published under the title *The Memories of Corporal Gheorghita*. *The Faded Flower* is a story of considerable size published the same year, and reveals the writer's epic talent. *Nicolae Manea's Note-book* (1907) reveals the writer's exceptional gift for psychological analysis in depicting the moral condition of his characters who start life with the firm intention of defending the loftiest ideals and end their wretched existence in some miserable provincial town. Then came *The Mud-Hut Dwellers* (1912) and a few other collections of tales; next the historical novel *The Soimaresti Family*, the social novel *A Mill Came Down the Siret* (Tales from the Banks of the Siret River) and *The Wonderful Grove, Tales for Children, Beyond the Mists, Ancuta's Inn, Under the Sign of the Cancer or The Reign of Prince Duca, The Axe, The Jderi Brothers*, etc. After the liberation of Rumania (August 23,

1944) Sadoveanu published *The Light Comes from the East, Moscow, Eastern Phantasies, Little Pauna, Mitrea Cocor, The Lure of the Flowers, Iron Bill and Nicoara Potcoava.*

Sadoveanu's work is pervaded by deep human sympathy, by the writer's boundless confidence in humble people, in their virtues, in the common man's high qualities which enable him by means of a relentless struggle to create a better life for himself. This is in fact that very essence of the robust optimism which characterizes Sadoveanu's works. His books arouse in the hearts of his readers love of life, confidence in the future, a hope that some day the cause of the people shall triumph. Sadoveanu's confidence in the people, in their future, has always been unshakable, and that is why his works constitute the chronicle of a past of struggle as well as a faithful mirror in which his readers see the reflection of age-long aspirations towards an ideal of freedom and justice.

Mihail Sadoveanu is the great poet in prose of Rumanian literature. Indeed, the artistic perfection of this writer reaches an unprecedented degree. One should particularly notice that Sadoveanu's literary language, drawing its sap from the language spoken by the people, the language of Neculce, the chronicler, and that of the famous Moldavian story-teller, Ion Creanga, is an instrument of rare beauty, handled by an artist whose mastery of style and command of the inexhaustible treasures of language mark Mihail Sadoveanu as one entitled to rank among the world's greatest writers.